The Old Boat Clubhouse

K.T. DADY

The Old Boat Clubhouse
Published by K.T. Dady

Copyright © 2023 K.T. Dady

Cover design by K.T. Dady.
Cover photography: Canva.

Take every opportunity. Go for it.

1

Jude

Jude Jackson rolled his aching shoulders over, trying to release some knots whilst waiting for the lift to come down to the hotel lobby. He caught a glimpse of himself in a nearby full-length mirror hanging on the wall and shook his head.

This has got to be the smallest hotel we've ever stayed in. Jeez, Keaton means business this time. Can't blame him. He's really messed things up for himself. Still, his new idea is a bit extreme, and God knows how he's going to pull this off. Knowing him, probably quite easily.

Jude figured it would be a nice vacation if nothing else. He'd never even heard of the Isle of Wight, but he thought it quite nice. He wanted to explore as soon as he got a chance. Sandly needed checking out, especially the long golden stretch of sand. It was summertime, and for that he was grateful. He wanted to surf. Relax a little. The journey over was intense. Keaton was intense.

Oh, why is this my life? I should take five to re-evaluate. There must be more to me than this crazy job.

He leaned a touch closer to the mirror to check the darkness beneath his eyes.

Wow! I didn't know I looked that bad. I seriously need some me-time. If Keaton's occupied for the next couple of hours, I'm heading straight for the sea. Even if there aren't any waves, I'm paddleboarding or something. I have to be in the water.

The lift door pinged open and Jude stepped inside. He scrunched his nose, breathing in the furniture polish recently applied to the shiny mahogany handrails around the walls. He turned and lowered his head, staring mindlessly down his legs towards his red trainers.

Ah, man, I've got to get out of these jeans.

No sooner had the door closed, than it opened again. Jude watched a young woman walk backwards into the small, enclosed area whilst pulling a double-tiered, chrome trolley. One of the wheels jammed. She tugged it hard, swore under her breath, and stumbled back straight into his chest. His hands jolted out on autopilot, grabbing her by the hips as he blew out wayward strands of her brown ponytail from his lips. His tired eyes widened as his left foot throbbed from contact with her black flats.

She quickly looked over her shoulder, and he could see small caramel flecks embedded in her sea-blue irises. Not that he was staring or anything.

'Oh, I'm so sorry.' She peeled herself from his body and took a slight step forward and to the side.

There wasn't anywhere else for either of them to stand, thanks to the housekeeping trolley.

'That's okay.' Jude could still taste something sweet from her hair. He wasn't quite sure what it was. Something tropical.

She glanced over her shoulder again. 'What is that accent, American or Canadian?'

Jude flashed his pearly whites, which had been straightened to perfection back in high school. 'I'm American.'

'Ooh, are you on holiday?'

'No, business trip.'

Sort of.

The real reason for his visit wasn't something he could disclose to housekeeping, unless she was the chosen one. If so, she'd find out soon enough. He stared at the back of her head and sighed quietly.

This is ridiculous. I can't believe I'm party to this. This is all Milly's fault. Her big ideas, winning Keaton over, yet again. She really wants my job. Look at this poor girl. I bet it's her. I wonder if she'll say yes.

Her light tropical scent and sea eyes swirled in his mind. The sooner he got out of this place the better. He was desperate to get to the water.

He watched her faffing around with mini bottles of shampoo sitting in a white box on the top tier and felt the need to say something. 'You worked here long?'

She brushed down the front of her peach hotel uniform. 'Five years now. Started when I was eighteen.'

Twenty-three, sweet, everyday job, seems friendly. Yep, Milly found the one.

'I guess that means you're from around here?'

'Yep, born and bred. Sandly till I die.' She snorted a laugh, which made him laugh. 'Where in America are you from?'

'California. I live in Malibu at the moment.'

'Ooh, like a Ken doll.'

He grinned, having been called that before.

Maybe I should dye out my sun-kissed locks. Lose my abs. Wait till she sees me with my surfboard. Ha!

'I tend to use the name Jude.'

She glanced his way again and smiled. 'Hey, Jude.'

His grin widened. 'Yeah.' If only he had a dollar for every time someone would *Hey, Jude* him. It was always worse when they felt the need to sing the song, something his mother was a fan of doing.

The lift door opened on the top floor, and he waited patiently for her to push the trolley out first.

He stepped onto the dark-red tweed carpet and looked over at the shiny oak door to his left. Right where she parked. For the first time since meeting her, he saw her face in full.

Sea glass eyes and thin lips sat perfectly in a love-heart face. A slight suntan captured her cheekbones, bringing the faintest of freckles to the surface across her button nose. Her dark hair was mostly in place in the black band clasping her thin locks, leaving a few around the front of her ears.

Jude shoved his hands into his pockets because they itched to place the loose strands behind her ears. Doing that to a stranger would also be considered weird in England, he figured. It was bad enough he couldn't stop smiling at her. 'What's your name?'

'Harriet. Hal, for short.'

He gave a slight nod. 'Good to meet you, Harriet. Hal, for short.'

She was smiling back but standing in his way of the hotel suite he wanted to enter.

He gestured behind her to the door.

'Oh.' She realised and tried to manoeuvre the trolley, but the rickety wheel was causing problems. She stopped struggling and looked up to meet his entertained gaze. 'Are you going in this room?'

'Uh-huh.'

'Oh, but I was told Keaton Byrd had checked in.'

'Yeah, he's my boss.'

Jude slid around her body and pulled out the keycard, entertained by how wide her eyes had stretched.

'So, it's true?' she asked, keeping her voice low. 'He's actually here in Sandly?'

'Yeah, for a few weeks.'

She tapped her chest as her face became even more animated. 'I've been sent back up here by him. I've already cleaned the suite. I was about to go home. Do you know what's wrong inside?'

I know exactly why he called you, but that's not for me to say.

'Nope.'

Harriet's jaw tightened, and a wave of nerves hit her eyes, and Jude suddenly felt the need to comfort her.

'You wanna come say hi?'

She didn't look as though she did.

'Hey, Harriet, it's okay. He won't bite.' He wasn't sure if his soft tones had steadied her somewhat, but she seemed to relax a little.

'I've never met a Hollywood film star before.'

Jude leaned over the trolley, trying not to lean too far forward whilst fighting off the guilty feeling seeping into his soul. 'He's just a guy.' He straightened and opened the door. 'Come on.'

Harriet wheeled her work trolley into the largest suite Hotel Royale had and parked it by the door. Her hands were still clamped tightly on the handle, and Jude could see her knuckles turning white.

Keaton Byrd was sitting on a faux-leather cream sofa over the other side of the room. His big dark eyes rolled up to peer over the top of pink-tinted John Lennon glasses as he shifted the tablet device perched on his knee, placing it on the glass table to his side.

Jude gestured towards Harriet. 'Housekeeping is here.'

Keaton relaxed back into his seat and smiled through his dark designer beard. He rubbed his hand over the short whiskers and narrowed his eyes, gaining some facial lines with the movement.

I can see his cogs turning from here. Now, how is he gonna play this. Hit hard, go for it? Maybe a soft tap will be

9

enough. Nah, he's a hitter. Always has been. He's gonna come out fighting.

Jude glanced sideways at Harriet.

The real question is, what are you gonna say?

Harriet swallowed hard enough for Jude to notice. 'Erm, is there something wrong with the room, Mr Byrd?'

Polite, professional, and in no way fangirling him. This is a good start.

Keaton pointed a blue-painted fingernail her way. 'How old are you?'

It was only natural Harriet looked confused. Jude didn't expect anything else.

'I... erm, I'm twenty-three.'

Keaton gave a slight nod of approval. 'That's okay.' He seemed to be talking to himself. 'Are you from around here?'

Harriet nodded. 'Yes, but what is this about? Do you need something cleaned?'

Keaton glanced at Jude as he breathed out a huff of an amused laugh. 'You could say that.'

I should step in, but he won't like my input yet. He needs to be in charge of this moment. Carry on, boss.

'Are you single?' asked Keaton.

Harriet's brow wrinkled.

Oh, man. She is so over these questions already.

Jude was half a second away from laughing out loud. The whole scene was so bizarre.

Harriet took a moment to reply. 'Why do you want to know that?'

Ooh, there's a snap in her voice. She won't be watching any more of his movies, that's for sure.

Keaton sat forward, resting on the edge of the sofa. 'Well, are you?'

Wow! He actually made that sound charming.

Jude saw Harriet take a controlled breath. Her right shoulder drooped a touch. Enough for him to notice, as he was still standing so close to her. Neither of them had time to move away from the door or each other before the interrogation had started.

'Yes,' she told him flatly. Her chin lifted and her jaw tensed. 'Now, what would you like me to clean?'

Keaton pointed at himself. 'My life.'

Enter stage left, me.

'We're looking to hire someone to work for Mr Byrd for a few weeks.'

'As his cleaner?'

'No. As a personal employee. You'll need to be discreet, sign an NDA, and in return, we'll pay you ten thousand. English pounds, that is. You will only be required for the short time we are here.'

Not sure what she's thinking, but judging by the slamming of hands on the hips, her gaping mouth, and that fierce laser beam about to shoot out of her eyes, I'd say my pitch didn't go down too well.

'I don't know what kind of hotel you think this is, Keaton Byrd and Surf Boy, but I'm not that sort of girl. If you want to pay someone to be your escort for your stay, then you're barking up the wrong tree asking me.'

Jude stumbled back into the wall as she pushed him out of her way, first with her elbow and then with the wheel of the trolley.

'Ow! No, wait. We weren't asking that.' Jude looked at his boss for backup, but Keaton was too busy being entertained by Harriet to bother to jump in and clear up the misunderstanding.

Harriet's eyes held nerves and evidence of an escape plan.

'Please, Harriet, let me explain properly.'

She folded her arms in a huff. 'Well?'

Crap! I can't tell her everything without her signing.

'Erm, I'm not sure if you saw the news a while back, but Keaton pretty much told a reporter he doesn't like people. He also told one of the major movie companies he'd never work for them again, and the money he promised to a children's charity kind of... bounced.' Jude cleared his throat and swallowed.

Harriet was now looking over at Keaton, and Keaton simply shrugged. 'What? I gave them the money in the end.'

Jude regained her attention. 'The point is, Keaton's image has taken a hit lately, which means work has slowed. So, we came here, on my assistant's advice, to... to, well, to settle Keaton down a bit.'

Keaton huffed and slumped back. 'I'm thirty-nine, Jude. You're making it seem like I'm an old man. Settle down, really?' He shook his head, then got up to pour himself half a glass of vodka.

'What has this got to do with me?' Harriet asked Jude.

Jude stepped closer to her trolley, holding on to the side. 'Milly, my assistant, has a cousin who lives here. She recommended the Isle of Wight because we were looking for somewhere outside of America that was quiet, homely, small town, that sort of thing. We're looking for a woman with matching qualities. We figured—'

Keaton interrupted, 'Someone from around here with not much ambition and little money would be able to step up and help make me look good.'

Andddd that's the end of that conversation. Well done, boss. I'm sure she's on board after that comment.

'What exactly do I have to do?' she asked, taking them both by surprise.

Keaton nodded at Jude, and he sprinted forward and opened a large leather bag slumped by the sofa. He pulled out some documents and waggled them at Harriet.

'Is that one of those I-can't-talk-about-Keaton-Byrd thingamajigs?' she asked knowingly.

Jude approached her, trying not to laugh. 'Yep.'

She eyed it with full-on suspicion. 'Is that all it is?'

He nodded her way, trying to show nothing but warmth and honesty. 'I promise.'

She flapped her fingers his way, staring only at the documents. 'Show me where to sign.'

'Really?'

Keaton huffed into his crystal glass. 'Jude. Pen.'

Jude quickly handed one over and much to his surprise Harriet signed the paperwork.

'Normally, we'd recommend you have a lawyer look that over first. Only—'

'Do I look like the type of person who has a lawyer? I'm not fussed about having to keep quiet about Keaton Byrd. I don't want to talk about his life anyway.'

Keaton raised his glass. 'Appreciate that.'

Jude had anxiety stuck in his throat he was sure should belong to her. 'Well, just so you know. There's no funny business in there. It's straightforward. We're not out to hurt anyone. This is about saving Keaton's reputation.'

A cold glare came his way. 'Can you get to the point now, please?'

'Erm, sure. So, basically, we want you to pretend to be Keaton's girlfriend while he's here.'

'Nope.'

'But—'

'Nope. I'm not prostituting myself out for—'

'You don't have to sleep with him.'

Harriet closed her mouth, and Jude took a breath.

'Look, Harriet, all we want is for the world to see Keaton has a nice, homely girlfriend. That he's not a complete ass… erm, cold and mean, like a lot of online trolls said. And that's putting it politely. This is about image only. You'll be seen in a few places together. Smile. Laugh. Hold hands, but that's as far as touching goes. You won't be alone. I'll be there, so will Milly, when she bothers to show up.' He huffed as he glanced at the door, half expecting her to appear.

'So, I'll be a fake date?'

'Exactly.'

'And you'll pay me ten thousand pounds just to do that?'

Keaton waggled his vodka at her. 'Don't even think about haggling. It's a good deal.'

'I wasn't going to. I do need to mention one thing though.'

Jude was the only one looking remotely interested. 'Yes?'

'I have a son.'

Keaton swung around. 'How old?'

'Seven.'

Keaton laughed out loud and raised his glass to the ceiling. 'Could life be any more perfect?' He turned to Jude. 'She should have haggled. The kid's a bonus. This is great. This, Jude Jackson, is going to work.'

Harriet shook her head, swishing her ponytail in the process. 'I don't want my boy in the papers.'

'No, that's cool,' said Jude quickly, before Keaton could intervene. 'We can arrange for his privacy.'

'Okay, then I'll do it.'

Keaton nodded his approval whilst Jude felt gobsmacked the crazy scheme was now a reality, and all within a matter of minutes.

Harriet gestured at the door. 'Can I go now? I need to get home.'

'Oh, sure.' Jude opened the door for her and tried to help with the trolley. He closed the door behind them and walked her the few steps back to the lift.

Harriet laughed out her shock. 'What just happened? I feel as if I'm in *Pretty Woman* or something.'

Jude smiled, hiding his nerves about the whole situation. 'Ah, well, at least you're not a prostitute.' He breathed out a nervous laugh as the lift door pinged open.

Harriet stepped inside and turned to face him. 'No, Jude. That would be your job. It would appear you're the only one who gets paid to kiss his arse.'

Jude's mouth gaped as the door closed, leaving him standing all alone wondering once again what the hell had happened to his life.

2

Harriet

Harriet Hadley sat upon the long wooden bench opposite her work locker. Everyone else in housekeeping had gone home, but she still hadn't changed out of her peach uniform.

So, that was weird. So weird.

She'd just signed some anti-talking document like the ones she'd seen on the crime shows her mum watched on the telly, and now she felt as though she was starring in one. And, bloody hell, she'd met Keaton Byrd, who she didn't rate much.

Do you really have to care about image when you're famous? Will I be suddenly famous?

She hoped not. All she was going to do was hang out with him for a few weeks. Then, he'd go home, and the reporters would make her fish and chip paper.

I can live with that. Ten grand. Yeah, I can definitely live with that. This cannot be real. How has this happened? I only came to work.

She stared mindlessly at her shoes, feeling a tad numb.

The door opened and in walked a suited young lady, who looked around Harriet's age. There was a hardness to her smile and not much in the way of friendliness going on in her dark eyes.

'Erm, can I help you?' asked Harriet. 'It's staff only in here.'

'You're the one I'm looking for.' She closed the door, swiped two fingers over the bench to check if it was clean, then sat close to Harriet. 'Hi, I'm Milly. I work for—'

'Keaton Byrd. Yeah, I know. Malibu Ken told me. You're his assistant, right?'

She scoffed slightly, then cleared her throat and straightened her slim shoulders. 'Well, I guess Jude is a bit like the doll. He definitely prefers swimwear and beaches. Sometimes I wonder why he's even in this job. He should be a lifeguard or something. Marine biologist, maybe.' She seemed to be talking to herself.

Harriet thought she'd bring the subject back to her, as that was obviously why Milly was there. She stared up at the woman's tight dark bun and wondered if she had a headache already. The back of her head was aching from her ponytail. She needed to get changed and go home. 'So, Milly, what can I do for you?'

Milly whipped out a green folder from her black satchel. 'Contract. Schedule. Expectations. All the details you'll need for the next few weeks. Shouldn't be hard for you. I've simplified everything.'

I guess that's her way of saying she thinks I'm a right thicko.

Milly pressed her hands onto the bag on her lap. 'I'd like to ask you some personal questions now, Harriet. I already know some stuff about you. I always do my research. I was the one who chose you.'

Harriet watched the woman's mouth struggle to curl up to a full-on smile. It seemed as though Milly wasn't used to smiling. One thing was for sure, she definitely thought highly of herself. The smugness in her tone revealed that much.

'I don't know who you have asked, but I'm pretty sure there wasn't much they could tell you about me. There isn't much to tell. I'm quite ordinary.'

'Good. That's exactly what's required. Mr Byrd's image needs a touch of ordinary.'

'He messed up bad, didn't he?'

'In many ways,' Milly mumbled. 'Right, so, back to you. When was the last time you had sex?'

Harriet choked on air. 'I'm sorry, what?'

Milly gave a firm nod. 'Sex. I need to know about your sex life.'

I don't have one, but blimming heck. Nosy much.

'It's not relevant.'

Milly moved her bag from her lap to place it by her feet. 'Yes, it is, Harriet. I need personal data. Mr Byrd's image is at stake. I can't parade you around until I know you are…' Her lips twisted to one side for a second.

'Are what?'

'Shall we say wholesome.'

Oh my goodness. That's the word she went with.

Milly seemed pleased with her choice, and Harriet was starting to think Hollywood people were nuts. Not that she cared. Ten grand was coming her way in a few weeks, which she could add to the money she was saving for a deposit to rent a flat. Finally, she'd be able to move out of her parents' house.

Okay, let's do this. It's surreal, and one hundred percent bizarre, but hey ho. When opportunity knocks, you have to open the door. Oh crap, this all my sister's fault, telling me to say yes to things. Oh well, here goes nothing.

'Seven years ago.'

Milly's eyes widened for a moment and then quickly went back to professional mode. She cleared her throat as she leaned down to her satchel to pull out an electronic notepad. 'So, seven years. Hmm.' She started to type. 'Have you had any boyfriends between then and now that you didn't sleep with?'

'Nope.'

Dark eyes held suspicion, but Harriet didn't care. She was going to answer Milly's personal questions truthfully. If Milly doubted her answers, well, that was her problem.

'Seriously, Harriet?'

'I've been busy, working and raising my son.'

Milly held her resting bitch face. 'But still. Come on, Harriet. We're all girls here. You can tell me if you made out with the whole football team. I won't judge. I have to know the truth so I can do damage control if need be. I also need to make sure you are right for this role. We can't hire anyone. And trust me, if you lie about anything, the press will find out, and they will slaughter you. Now is not the time for lies or sugar-coating.'

'I'm not lying. I don't know why it's so hard to believe. I don't think everyone around the world has sex every day, week, or year. There are probably loads of people who go long periods of time without that kind of interaction.'

Milly almost let loose a sympathetic smile as she asked, 'Don't you want a boyfriend?'

'No. The last one put me off.'

'Not all men are the same.'

'I know, but after getting pregnant at sixteen, having to listen to my boyfriend tell me he didn't want me or the baby, watch him sail away on the four o'clock ferry to the mainland, and feeling scared out of my wits about my body and life, I never wanted to date again.'

'Is it really scary being pregnant?'

'It was for me. I was so young and frightened by what was happening to me. The first time the baby kicked, I cried from fear alone. I didn't know what to expect. Nobody does their

19

first time, but I think it's worse when you're still a kid yourself. Plus, I was sad. That didn't help. I wasn't one of those who enjoyed pregnancy. I had my family for support, but it's still lonely when you don't have a partner holding your hand. I would see happy couples and...' She took a deep breath.

That's enough of that.

'I don't ever want kids. People think that's weird,' said Milly quietly.

'I'm not going to lie. I would like a nice boyfriend. I'm not opposed to a bigger family, but I thought my son's dad was nice, and, well, look how that turned out.'

'Will he be a bother to us?'

'I doubt it. I think he lives in Wales. I don't know. I haven't heard from him since the day he left me when I was pregnant. I get told snippets of info from others every so often, and I have to tell them I'm not interested.'

'Your face will be in the news once word gets out Keaton Byrd is dating you. There's every chance your ex will rock up. They often do. There's money in it for them if they tell their story of their time with you.'

'There's not much to tell. Besides, it will hardly make him look good.'

'They usually lie to make themselves look good.'

'There's nothing I can do about that.'

'Okay, well, at least I know about him.'

Flipping heck. What if he does write about me in the papers for a few quid? I can't focus on that. Ten grand. Tommy. Our own place to live. Just focus on that, Hal.

Milly smiled her own struggle of a smile. 'I think you're perfect for this role, Harriet. You're young, pretty, practically a virgin. You have a low-paid job, you're a single parent, and you seem... sweet. Do you have a police record?'

'No.'

'Addictions?'

'No.'

'Unusual hobbies?'

'I swim in the sea every morning before work and again after I pick my kid up from school. Does that count?'

'No. What about your family? Tell me about them.'

'Erm, well, Tommy is your average seven-year-old. My parents, Ronnie and Fiona, are really boring. Dad's a cab driver, and when he's not working, you can find him in the garden. He likes to talk plants or Southampton football team. That's where he's from, Southampton. My mum's from here. She works part-time in a supermarket. I've always lived at home with them. I have five sisters.'

'Ooh, five. I have one younger brother. I always wanted a sister. I bet it was fun growing up in your house.'

Yeah, I guess it was. Apart from the fights, hormones, antics, and non-stop noise...

'It was okay. My sister Kerri still lives at home with us. She has a baby and is a uni student, but her partner will be finding them somewhere to call home soon. Well, his parents are working on it. They have a bit of money.'

'What about your other sisters?'

'Our Molly lives with her boyfriend over in Pepper Bay. That's the place next door. She works in a tea shop and a pub. Her boyfriend is a chef. So, no scandal there. Our eldest, Grace, is the only one married. She works at a donkey rescue centre and is a part-time photographer. Her husband is a doctor at our local hospital. He's Canadian. Ashley is a jeweller. She makes personal bits and pieces using crystals and beads. More arts and crafts than diamonds and pearls, but she likes to call herself a jeweller.'

'What about the last sister. I only counted four.'

Oh, you don't miss a trick. Okay, well, not sure how you're going to like these apples but...

'Lexi owns a flower shop. She also writes books.'

Milly's perfect eyebrows lifted a touch. 'Oh, what genre does she write?'

'Erotic romance.'

Harriet couldn't be sure if that bothered Milly or not. Her facial expressions were few. She mostly looked as though you were in her way and she was late.

'I guess her sales will improve.'

Harriet never thought about how her actions might affect her family, but then again, she hadn't done much thinking at all since the moment she stepped on Jude's foot in the lift. 'Erm, Milly. I'm going to have to tell my family the truth. I can't pretend to them. Not about something like this.'

Milly tapped her manicured pink fingertips upon her legs. 'It's only for a few weeks.'

'It's going to get crazy though, isn't it?'

'We've hired our own photographer for the promo. We're hoping we might have at least a week before the whole world knows where Keaton Byrd is.'

Harriet snorted out a laugh. 'This is Sandly. Trust me, everyone here already knows. We weren't sure if it was a tall tale at first. I thought maybe he was filming. Anyway, it'll be all over the Isle of Wight by lunchtime.'

'Joy.'

'So, can I tell my family? They'll think it's weird me suddenly dating some film star.'

'There's nothing weird about it, Harriet. Somebody has to date movie stars. They're humans too.'

'I didn't mean it like that. I just want my family to know the truth. They won't tell. We're very tight.'

'I'm sure, but they'll still have to sign an NDA.'

'Okay. What about Tommy? Would it be okay if I told him you, Keaton, and Jude are my new friends and we're hanging out for a while? He'll get on board with that.'

'Sure, but kids tend to hear stories at school.'

'He'll believe me, not them.'

Milly huffed out what appeared to be frustration. 'Well, that's a lot of people you want in on this, Harriet. I'm not sure it will work out that way. We were hoping for discretion.'

'My family can be discreet.'

There was another huff and puff of fresh minty air coming from Milly's mouth. 'Fine. But if they break the contract, your family will be sued for a hell of a lot of money. Do you understand? I mean it, Harriet. This is top-level serious. Our lawyers don't play games, and they certainly have no sympathy. Can you really trust everyone in your circle to keep their mouths shut about this? We're talking about a lot of people here.'

If she's trying to scare me, she's doing a good job. I don't know what to do now. That's a lot of responsibility I'll be putting on my family. Perhaps it's best they don't know till it's over. Oh, flipping heck.

As though reading her mind, Milly added, 'The less people know, the better. Plus, it's only a few weeks. Tell your family the same thing you're going to tell your son, and when the press splash the news everywhere, tell them it's reporters blowing everything out of proportion. Say you simply volunteered to show us around town because Mr Byrd wanted a local to give him a tour while here.'

'You think my family will believe that?'

'Oh, honey, you'd be surprised what people believe. It's my job to make Keaton Byrd look good, and by the end of his trip here, everyone will believe the man is a saint.'

Harriet scoffed. 'Hardly. He'll have dated a small-town girl for a few weeks. I don't know how much of an impact that will make.'

Milly's eyes held the slightest of twinkles. 'Oh, you'll see.'

Wow, she reminds me of the snake out of The Jungle Book. *She's definitely got game-plan written all over her face. Oh, crumbs, what on earth did I sign up for?*

3

Jude

Mid-evening was every bit as beautiful as the sun-filled morning in Sandly. Jude stood on the long stretch of golden sand, staring out at the calm sea glittering as though diamonds had recently fallen from the sky to float upon the tips of the water. He glanced down at his red-and-white paddleboard and then around him to see a handful of people taking advantage of the warm weather and beautiful beach. He was the only one wearing a wetsuit. It was his summer one, short sleeves and short legs, revealing a golden suntan that seemed a different shade to those he could see around him.

He glanced back at the line of colourful beach huts up by the promenade, finding the one he had hired for his stay, checking the nautical-themed hut was locked. He caught sight of Harriet Hadley as she made her way across the sand with a small boy in tow.

I'm guessing that's her son. And they're heading right for me. Perhaps she's got something she wants to clear up before her new job starts tomorrow. Why is she smiling like that? Ah, I get it. She thinks I'm a cliché surfer dude.

'Hi.'

Harriet stopped at the tip of his paddleboard. 'Hello.' She looked down at the dark-haired lad, who looked like her but with more freckles. 'Tommy, this is Jude. My new friend I was telling you about.'

Big blue eyes bore straight into Jude, making him swallow hard, not knowing what was coming next.

'Is this yours?' asked Tommy, reaching down to touch the board.

'Yeah. You ever been on a paddleboard before?'

Tommy giggled, revealing tiny dimples in both cheeks. 'Yes, with my old water sports teacher. And I've been on a surfboard, and a bodyboard, and a jet ski.'

'Wow, you really love your water sports, huh?'

Tommy shrugged and lowered his gaze. 'Yeah. I miss it all.'

Jude glanced at Harriet before turning his attention back to Tommy. Before either of them could speak, he asked, 'If you miss it, why did you stop?'

Harriet cleared her throat, but Tommy was already talking.

'Pete, my teacher, has left to go travelling for a few years, and Mum can't afford the lessons that are at another beach way over there.' He flapped one arm over his head. 'But it's okay. She's saving to get me my own surfboard, then I can practise by myself.'

The embarrassment in her eyes didn't go unnoticed. She was now avoiding Jude's face altogether and staring out to sea instead.

Tommy added, 'Mum still takes me swimming here after school. I'm only allowed in the shallow part, and she swims by my side. She doesn't need to. I can swim on my own.'

Without looking away from the water, Harriet told her son he wasn't old enough to swim in the sea by himself.

Tommy let out a big sigh and then beamed his smile straight back at Jude. 'Are you a water sports teacher?'

'Erm, no. But there isn't anything about water sports I don't know. Trust me, kid, I've been practically living in the ocean since I was younger than you.'

Tommy giggled, which brought Harriet's attention back to Jude.

Jude smiled warmly, then gestured towards his board. 'You two fancy a ride?'

Tommy was already jumping up and down before Harriet could even open her mouth.

Jude scanned her summer wetsuit, trying not to make it look as though he were eyeing up her body. He totally was, but thought he hid that well by pointing out they were dressed for the occasion.

'We're dressed for a swim in the sea,' she told him flatly.

'You got sunscreen on?'

And I said that why? Like she's an idiot who doesn't know what she's doing.

He glanced over at the sea, checking out the movement, the danger levels, and if there were any rips. All pretty standard stuff he knew to do before heading out.

'We've got sun cream,' said Tommy, now stroking the board and giving his mum puppy-dog eyes.

'We can stay shallow,' said Jude. 'You can stay seated. There's plenty of room.'

'Please, Mum.'

Jude watched her mulling it over. Her thin lips twisted slightly to one side as her left hand twirled her ponytail.

'Okay,' she finally said, making one little boy very happy, and Jude as well.

Tommy immediately grabbed the board and Jude joined him, helping to place its large frame on the water. Harriet climbed on behind her son whilst Jude kept them steady.

'I don't want to sit down, Mum.'

Harriet held his waist. 'You can stand in a minute. Let's get out first.'

27

Jude smiled at them both, secretly loving having some company on his board. He'd seen others sharing before but had never experienced it himself. There was an old man back home who went out every day on a paddleboard with his large black dog on board. The dog even had his own life jacket.

The warmth of the sun wasn't the only thing relaxing Jude. Being on the water brought out a side to him that was beyond chilled. Everything about the sea took him into a zen zone he wished he could live in forever. When he glanced behind him at Tommy, he could see the boy felt the same way.

Harriet looked up at him watching her son. 'He's always been a water baby.'

Jude stared back out at the sea. 'Oh, I hear that.' He glanced back as they bobbed upon a calmer, flatter surface. 'You wanna paddle, Tommy?'

Tommy's big grin was brighter than the sun as Harriet helped him to his feet. Jude handed over the paddle and Tommy knew what to do straight away.

Jude laughed. 'You definitely need a junior size.'

'Mum said, if all goes well, I should have my surfboard for Christmas. Maybe I can get a paddleboard for my birthday. That's a good idea, Mum. Keep that in mind.'

Jude gave her a sympathetic smile, knowing full well how expensive paddleboards were. Harriet was keeping quiet, and he was wondering what was going through her mind.

I could buy him one today, but I somehow think she won't go for that. Shame. Summer has just started here. Perhaps she's going to sort it herself as soon as we pay her. I hope he gets what he wants for the water. I know exactly how he feels about being out here.

Harriet was staring at the shore, and he wondered if she wanted to be back there. Away from him, possibly.

Jude offered his hand over her shoulder, gesturing for her to stand up in the middle. He smiled warmly as her slim fingers slipped into his.

She glanced back at him. 'It's so peaceful out here.'

'Yep. To me, it's the best part of the planet.'

'And it's a beautiful evening.'

'It sure is.' He looked back at the beach. 'It's really nice here.'

Harriet muffled her laugh. 'Have you fallen in love with the island already?'

The smell of salty air mingled with the slight waft of sweetness coming from her hair every so often. He silently inhaled deeply, breathing her in just because he could. Because he wanted to. Because very soon, madness would ensue and he wouldn't have this moment again. He didn't answer her question, but he did place his hands upon her shoulders for a split second when a wave rolled beneath them.

Harriet lowered her head and laughed. 'I'm okay, Jude.'

He watched as her son turned to give her a go with the paddle. They started talking and giggling about something, both looking so happy and relaxed, and something shifted inside of Jude. A stirring he couldn't quite fathom.

I'm not sure you'll be okay soon. Keaton's crap starts tomorrow. I don't think you're gonna know what's hit you. I'm not sure I'm comfortable with this anymore. Look how at peace they are. What if we destroy that? And for what? Keaton Byrd's image.

He smiled as she turned to face him. 'We're taking over your paddleboard. Here.' She offered back the paddle.

He folded his arms, gaining her attention to that part of his body. She was staring at his forearms for quite some time. He tried not to allow the smile to build on his face, but it was damn near impossible. He cleared his throat, and she met his gaze. 'You keep the paddle, Hal. I don't mind being a man of leisure for a bit.'

She bit her bottom lip and grinned. 'So, that's the real reason we're here.'

'Oh, yeah. I always wanted my own staff. Hey, look, now I have two water chauffeurs.'

She looked over his shoulder as she steered them in line to the shore. 'Milly reckons you should have some sort of sea job.'

'Huh! She would. She's been after my job ever since she started.'

'How much do you love your job with Keaton?'

Now there's a question and a half.

'It's okay.'

Harriet raised her dark eyebrows, giving the impression she wasn't buying that statement. 'But you'd prefer to be out here.'

His eyes found hers, and suddenly there was more going on than his mouth smiling. A fluttering in his solar plexus would sum it up, but he was ignoring the flapping rhythm. 'I guess it would be my dream job.'

'You could be a water sports teacher. How much do you know?'

He laughed. 'Everything. I can windsurf, water ski, you name it. I even had my own boat once. That was back before I started working for Keaton. And when I became his PA, I didn't have a lot of time to myself for the first couple of years, so I ended up selling. Not gonna lie. I shed a tear saying goodbye to that boat.'

Harriet playfully tapped his shoulder.

Jude shrugged, putting his arms behind his back for a moment to hide the goosebumps her touch had caused. 'Hey, I loved my boat. Wasn't anything fancy. Small but mine.'

Her gaze dreamily met the land. 'Small but mine. I like that. That's how I feel about where I live.'

'You ever thought about leaving?'

'Nope. Never.'

He watched her hand the paddle to her son. Milly had well and truly picked the right woman for the job, but how was Harriet going to cope with so much change? The way she looked at her home told him how happy and settled she was.

A strange protectiveness powered through him, taking him by surprise. He would have to make sure she was safe and happy at all times. There was no way he would let Milly or Keaton overrule her. He could sense her vulnerability, or maybe it was his own. Time would tell who would come off worse.

I'm gonna be there with you, Harriet Hadley. Every step of the way. I'm actually not looking forward to this at all. It feels so different now real people are involved.

She suddenly leaned over towards him, almost resting her head on his chest. She balanced herself as her hand came up to cover half her face. 'The Donkey Sanctuary tomorrow.' She grinned widely, causing him to smile back.

'First date.'

She shrugged nonchalantly. 'Could be worse.'

He locked eyes with her, knowing full well what he was doing but unable to control himself any longer. Well, maybe he could. He just didn't want to. He already liked sinking into the ocean he could see every time he looked her way. 'Could be better.'

She held his gaze for a moment, glanced at his mouth, and then turned back to her son.

Jeez, what the hell. This woman is giving me butterflies. Great! Okay, reel it in, Jackson. This can't happen.

Harriet looked over her shoulder, flashing the most amazing smile. Everything about her was alert and alive, filled with sunshine, sea, and freedom of the outdoors.

Okay, looks like it's happening.

4

Harriet

Normally after work Harriet would go straight home, maybe get on with some housework or do some shopping, or sometimes she'd have lunch with one of her sisters or stay at the hotel and have a discounted lunch with her work colleagues. Not today. Milly had sent for her to have lunch in Keaton's suite, and Harriet had happily munched away on one of Hotel Royale's finest burgers whilst Milly banged on about schedules, expectations, and fake dates.

She discovered Keaton Byrd had a much larger entourage back home, but Milly thought it best if only a small circle bombarded the Isle of Wight. So, Jude also had the chauffeur job for their rebranding trip.

He opened the car door for Harriet to step out at the car park of the Donkey Sanctuary. Her white pumps scrunched onto the gravel as she glanced up to notice Jude staring at the hemline of her blue summer dress, where it sat below her knees. He lowered his sunglasses from his head to sit upon his nose and looked the other way.

Was he checking out my legs? Surely not. Although, he did hold the slightest blush when I caught him looking. He's hiding behind his sunglasses now. Coward. Oh, don't laugh, Hal.

'Car park looks empty,' said Milly, turning her nose up towards the sky. 'What is that smell?'

'Donkeys,' replied Harriet, grinning at Jude.

Milly raised one foot to adjust the strap of her wedged sandals. 'Eww, they smell like they need a bath.'

A man in his fifties got out of the car and surveyed the area as though he were about to redesign the place. He sniffed loudly whilst rubbing a hand over his long grey beard, letting out a faint groan. 'I'm glad it's empty. It'll be better for us if there are less people.'

Harriet turned to Keaton's private photographer, Warren. 'It's midweek. Plus, the kids are in school, so, yeah, it'll be pretty quiet. Depends how many tourists decide to holiday here in June.'

Milly's head whooshed her way. 'Do you get many tourists in June?' Before Harriet could answer, she added, 'We were hoping you wouldn't.'

'It's summer season now,' said Harriet, watching Keaton lazily exit the car. 'That's when they start pouring in, but it's at its busiest during the school holidays.'

'Oh, when does that start?' asked Milly, clearly concerned.

'End of July.'

Milly almost smiled at Keaton. 'Good. We'll be long gone by then.'

And I won't miss you one bit.

Harriet looked at Jude's firm back muscles. His lemon polo shirt did little to hide his fitness.

I might miss you.

Keaton was reading the old wooden welcome sign by the entrance. 'Milly, make sure we leave a decent donation to this place.'

Milly already had her electronic notebook out. 'Yes, sir. On that.'

Harriet was sure Jude rolled his eyes beneath his sunglasses as he glanced over his shoulder. She stepped closer to him and went to speak but got distracted by her sister staring at her from the entrance.

And so it begins.

Harriet gestured towards the doorway. 'Come on. I'll introduce you to Grace. She's my eldest sister. She works here, and she's looking straight at us.'

'Uh-huh,' said Keaton. 'I see her. Oh, she's cute.'

'She's married,' said Harriet quickly, leading them towards her intrigued sister. 'Hello, Grace,' she sung out, trying for normal and knowing full well there wasn't anything normal about turning up at a donkey sanctuary with a Hollywood film star.

Grace looked at each person in turn before directing all her attention back onto Harriet.

Harriet cleared her throat to speak, but Keaton got in first.

'You must be the delightful Grace. Harriet has told me all about you.' He shook her hand whilst she gawped at him. 'Your sister said this should be the first place we visit on the island.' He started to lead a gobsmacked Grace away, swiftly followed by Warren.

Milly kept their pace whilst Harriet and Jude lagged behind.

Jude bent closer to Harriet's ear. The warmth of his breath causing a tingle in her stomach. 'Hey, how you holding up so far?'

She felt a tad disappointed when he straightened. 'Easy-peasy at the moment.' She tried not to laugh but a small one escaped, sounding like a strangled giggle.

Jude chuckled. 'Early days.'

'Yes, but it's not going to look good if he starts hitting on my sister.'

'Don't worry, Warren will only capture the moments Keaton is draped over you.'

Harriet stopped walking, and Jude quickly reached for her elbow. 'Hey, I didn't mean it like that. He won't drape. I promise. Perhaps a holding-hands picture to seal the deal. That's as far as it will go. You have my word.'

Harriet was fully aware Jude witnessed a huge sigh leave her mouth. She didn't care. Deflated before the race had even started was exactly how she was feeling. Motivation was needed. She had to get her head in the game. Act out her part. Claim her prize. Just hold the man's hand.

There will be women all over the world who would give anything to do just that. I'm not one of them. Why do I want to hold Jude's hand? Stop looking at his hand, Hal. For crying out loud. Act normal.

She remained fixed on his large sun-kissed knuckles, and another sigh left her as she made her way back along the pathway to see the donkeys and, no doubt, have her picture taken.

Grace pulled her to one side as soon as she could. 'What the bloody hell, Hal!'

There were only three people in the world who had the ability to make Harriet feel like a ten-year-old, and her eldest sister was one of them. She sank slightly into her shoulders and attempted a smile, but it came out weak and lopsided, as it always did whenever she tried to lie. 'I met them at the hotel. Keaton Byrd asked me to show him around the island. He wanted someone local.'

'And now the part where he's having photos done with you. Harriet, he held your hand.'

I know. It was so bizarre. Me and my big ideas. It's all Lexi's fault, with her say-yes-to-things speech she laid on me the other month. Why am I doing this mad thing? Ten grand, that's why. Right. Focus.

'I think he likes me, Grace.'

Grace's blue eyes seemed to darken in the sunlight. 'You know he put his hand low on my back. And I mean low. I had to politely wriggle away. And I don't see why I had to be polite about it. He's lucky I didn't bite his head off.'

'Oh, he's the tactile type.'

Grace brushed over the top of her highlighted-blonde hair, swishing back the escaped wispy bits. 'He'll be the floored type if he tries that with me again. Good thing Charlie isn't here.'

Harriet thought about her brother-in-law. She was glad he wasn't around to see Keaton's wandering hands either. It wouldn't have ended well.

Grace almost scowled, which was so unlike her. She had a kind face that rarely gave off horrible vibes. 'I hope you know what you're playing at, Hal.'

Harriet huffed at being spoken to that way. 'I do.'

Grace turned on her heels but not before she quickly added, 'And this better not affect Tommy.'

Harriet's fists clenched so tightly, she left fingernail imprints in her palms.

Ooh, how dare she. Of course I won't let this affect Tommy. I'm not completely stupid, Grace, but thanks. Oh, how much longer do we have to be here? I'm fed up already, and I've got another three weeks left.

She sighed deeply, trying to control her racing thoughts and pumped heart. Then, a calming presence surrounded her.

'Hey, Hal.'

She turned slowly to look at Jude full on. His smile was as warm as ever, and his laid-back persona was shining through.

'You ready to go home, ma'am?'

'Oh, does it show on my face?'

He gave a half-shrug. 'You kind of look lost.' He glanced over her shoulder before returning to her face. 'Hey, you wanna hang out at the beach later?'

'I take Tommy for a swim after school. You could swim with us, if you like.'

'I like.'

She chewed on her lip, simply to stop a wide smile. There was no way she was showing him some soppy, doe-eyed look. She wasn't sure how well she was doing with that, because he was grinning at her, and now he had removed his sunglasses, she could see something looking like more than friendship.

'How old are you, Jude?'

'Twenty-seven.'

'That's a good age to buy another boat.'

She watched the creases appear around his eyes. 'You think?'

'Yes,' she whispered. 'I do.'

You could moor it in Sandly Harbour.

They held each other's stare until Milly approached, then they both turned in opposite directions to pet some donkeys.

5

Jude

Helping Harriet flank Tommy in the sea made Jude feel extremely responsible for once. He had the feeling that was how his water sports instructor felt giving lessons to kids. He kept a close eye on the boy, constantly worried he might drown at any given moment. He knew he was overthinking. They had Tommy covered. Plus, the kid could swim, and Harriet was just as impressive in the water. But still, he was taught to always have his wits about him in the sea. He was surprised by the lack of lifeguards, but confident in his own life-saving abilities, as that was part of the course for him growing up.

Jude's old teacher was never far from his mind when he was at sea. Seeing Tommy take on the water like a junior Olympic swimmer settled his nerves a touch.

He wondered how hard it would be to have such a job. Could that be something he could do? He held all the relevant certificates. How different his life would be. It was definitely tugging at his mind, and especially the boat comment Harriet had made earlier in the day at the Donkey Sanctuary. It wasn't as though he couldn't afford another boat. He was so tempted and hadn't stopped thinking it over.

Every time he was in the sea, his whole thought process changed. Even back home. It was the only place he felt he truly belonged. Now, Harriet was tempting him, and not just with her words.

He followed them back onto the sand and sat by their sides on large towels, drying off beneath the brightness of the sun.

Tommy spotted one of his friends and ran off to play, leaving behind a moment of silence only interrupted by the cry of seagulls and the whooshing sound of the waves meeting the shore.

Jude kept his eye on the boys in the near distance, bouncing around an inflatable ball. 'He's a good kid.'

Harriet nodded. 'Hmm, he is. He's happy, and that's important.'

Is she trying to tell me something? She's not making eye contact. I guess if she has something to say, she'll say it soon enough.

'Island life seems nice.'

'I love it, Jude. This is a great place to raise a kid. I don't think anyone in my family will ever leave. We've all been so happy here.'

He watched her intently until she met his gaze.

'How about you? Are you happy, Jude?'

What a question.

'I guess. Not much to complain about. I have no angst in my life.' He grinned widely, flashing his teeth. 'I've always been happy. I grew up in a happy family. I like my life.'

Except my job.

'Are your family water babies like you?'

Jude breathed out a laugh through his nose. 'No. God, no. My parents are lawyers, and so is my sister. We always lived close to the water, but I was the only one to gravitate that way. My dad says he doesn't have time for water sports. Believe me, I've tried to coax him to the beach. He's what's known as a workaholic.'

'Working for someone like Keaton Byrd must be hard for you. I can't imagine being around him full-time. His life seems so bizarre.' She shifted on her towel so she was facing him. 'When do you think the reporters will turn up?'

'We were hoping for some private time for at least a week, but we've been out and about now. The local press will be on you first, probably starting tomorrow, and then the international press. Milly will put out Keaton's donkey love tonight, then, by morning, the world will know Keaton Byrd is here.'

'Wow!'

He leaned closer, placing a hand on her knee, and then quickly removed it, hoping he didn't make his mindless manoeuvre awkward. 'Hey, it'll be okay.'

Her face showed signs of concern she couldn't hide. 'I've seen the way they swarm people on the telly.'

'And that's why I'm here. It's my job to protect you, Hal. I won't let them sweep you away.'

'Is that why you came swimming with us?'

'What? No. I… I wanted to, that's why.'

'Are you supposed to be around me all the time? It's okay. You can tell me the truth.'

'That is the truth. I'm here because this is where I want to be.'

Jeez, she thinks I'm her bodyguard. I guess I am, of sorts, but that's not why I'm with her. I like being around her. I'm not getting into it.

The sound of a few nearby people filled the gap between them whilst Jude thought about his hand on her knee. He hoped he didn't blush as he casually pulled it away. Raking his fingers through his hair and pulling in his lips, he stared over at Tommy.

41

'Do you want to get something to eat with us in a bit?' asked Harriet, making him jump slightly. She gestured over to the beach huts. 'There's the burger bar over the road. I promised Tommy he could have junk food today.'

Jude was taken aback by the sudden offer to hang out with them again.

It's not an actual date, is it? No. She didn't ask me out. She's just being polite. Why am I even dissecting this? She asked. I'm going. Simple.

'Yeah, I'm up for that. You know, tomorrow night you'll have to have dinner out somewhere with Keaton.'

He watched her sigh whilst twiddling the corner of the towel. 'Yeah, I know. Milly told me. She's doing some sort of intense search for places we can be seen at. I know some nice restaurants, but she shut down my ideas. Reckons she knows what she's looking for.'

'Maybe you can show me some of the places you know. I'd like to check them out while I'm in town. I trust your judgement.'

Harriet checked on her son, smiled to herself, and then nodded. 'Okay. There's a lovely fish restaurant over by the harbour. I think you'll like it.'

'Sounds great.'

A few beats later, Harriet cleared her throat. 'It has a nice view of all the boats. The harbour.'

He pretended he didn't see her blush. He daren't stay too long staring at her face anyway. Those faint freckles, the sweep of sun across her nose, sea eyes, and that tropical scent. His mind needed to be somewhere else.

The boats. The harbour. She's making me think about sailing again. Is she doing this on purpose for some reason? Nah, probably not. I guess she's figured me out. I'm not hard to get to know. Just show me the water and I'm at peace. A restaurant by the sea is totally the kind of place where I would choose to eat. I'm looking forward to going.

Jude felt happy. A nice meal out with Harriet was on the cards and he couldn't wait. He gestured towards the huts. 'Shall we get changed?'

Harriet grinned, looking as though she was glad of the change of subject and having something else to focus on. 'Are you ready for burger and chips already?'

'Chips? Oh, you mean fries. Yeah, I'm hungry now.'

She stuck her fingers in her mouth and gave a short sharp whistle that made him jump but also gained Tommy's attention. He laughed to himself as he plodded across the sand to his hired beach hut to get out of his wetsuit.

Tommy was ready the quickest, and Jude spent his time waiting for Harriet to get changed by reading the names on the paving beneath his feet. The whole of the promenade was lined with etched words. He called through the closed door of the beach hut. 'Hey, Hal, these plaques out here are pretty cool. Have you got one?'

Her faded voice called back. 'No. It's mostly tourists who buy them. The money goes back into the town. Helps with the upkeep.'

Jude brushed his trainer over an engraved name that said something about someone called Primrose and a merman. 'I wanna get one,' he mumbled to himself.

What could mine say? Jude Jackson. Isle of Wight. Fell in love with...

Harriet came outside, sporting shorts and a baggy pink tee-shirt. Her shoulder-length brown hair was loosely tied at the nape of her neck, and a trace of sunshine lined her hairline.

He couldn't help but stare. The sea glass and faint freckles were captivating him once again. Her face was fresh and healthy, and he thought Harriet Hadley held a natural glow that made her features look as pure as a Disney princess. One who loved to paddleboard and swim.

'You're staring at me, Jude.'

'Hmm, oh, erm…' He met her amused expression, bit his lip, and smiled. 'Yeah, I guess I was.'

They shared another one of those moments where they simply looked into each other's eyes and nobody moved.

'You look nice, Hal. Pink suits you,' was all he could think to say.

She reached out and touched his salmon-coloured shirt. 'Kind of suits you too.'

He was sure that's what she said, but he could have misheard. His mind was busy concentrating on the fact she had her hand on his chest, right over his rapidly beating heart. He swallowed hard, placed one hand over hers, and went to speak, then his phone rang, breaking eye contact.

The moment was gone, and they parted so he could take the call. He glanced her way whilst Milly spoke loudly in his ear, giving him a headache, as she failed to get to the point straight away. He finally got off the phone and smiled weakly. 'Pictures are out already.'

'What does that mean?'

'It means it's showtime.'

'Can we pretend it's not yet and go and have our dinner?'

He breathed out a hushed laugh and nodded. 'Well, we can try.'

Harriet waved Tommy over with one hand as she zipped up her beach bag with the other. 'I'm pretty sure we won't be tracked down in the burger bar.'

'Oh, you'd be surprised.'

She straightened, flung her bag over her shoulder, grabbed his arm, and tugged him away. 'Come on.'

He quickly pulled back. 'Erm. It's best if we don't do that.'

She looked mortified, as though he had dumped her, and a thump hit him straight in the gut.

'The contract,' he murmured, so Tommy couldn't hear. He tried to take her bag to carry it for her, but she tugged it back to her shoulder.

'I understand.' Her voice was soft and almost broken and it hit him with a second shot, this one straight to the heart.

'I'm sorry,' he felt the need to add as they crossed the road.

She walked past him as he opened the door for them to enter the burger bar. 'It's okay, Jude. Really.'

It's not. It is so not. You wanted to hold my arm, and I wanted that too, and I yanked it away, like a complete jerk. I would happily walk anywhere with you on my arm. Hell, I would hold your hand. Great! This is getting better and better. I can't like this woman. I just can't. Come on, man, get a grip.

No sooner than they were seated, a young girl excitedly approached Harriet. 'OMG, Hal. You're trending.' She slowly gave Jude the once over. 'Who's Hot Stuff?'

Whilst Jude was mulling over the fact he'd been called Hot Stuff by a girl who looked to still be in school, Hal had quickly answered.

'Keaton Byrd's bodyguard.' And then she ordered food as though everything was perfectly normal.

6

Harriet had never worn a ball gown before, with the exception of a bridesmaid dress for Grace's wedding, but that was different to what she had been clothed in by Milly.

Milly had faffed and moaned about the lack of entourage and had explained that Harriet would look a million dollars if Keaton's team was around.

Harriet didn't mind. She thought she looked quite magical and wondered where on the island would warrant such glamour. It turned out to be a restaurant called Swan Lake.

The whole of the Hadley family had only ever embarked on the 1930s style eatery once, back when Grace hit thirty. It wasn't Harriet's cup of tea. She preferred the less formal approach to eating out.

It was weird having everyone staring at her. She didn't feel comfortable putting any of the fancy food into her mouth whilst people watched from the other tables. What if someone whipped out their phone and took an action shot? Washing machine mouth was not the look she was hoping for if and when her face hit the front page.

Keaton seemed perfectly at home. He gave a few smiles here and there and was polite to the starstruck staff, and his acting skills were on point. Whenever he was pretending to be totally in love with Harriet, even she almost believed him.

She tried so hard to make the scene appear real, but it wasn't easy, especially as her eyes kept wandering across the room to see what Jude was up to.

Jude and Milly looked like the FBI. They even had earpieces in and seemed to be communicating using their own secret code. Jude had the arched entrance covered, and Milly was standing over by the doorway that led to the toilets.

There was a tall, lean man happily playing the restaurant's grand piano, and even he earned himself a few stern glares from Milly for doing absolutely nothing wrong.

Flipping heck, anyone would think Keaton's the president. Jude's got the bodyguard vibe going on, but I think it's Milly everyone should be worried about. I swear, if one person dares approach our table, I think she'll floor them. And she won't care. This could be the weirdest moment of my life.

Her gaze locked with Jude's for a second, but he quickly cut off contact by scanning the room once more.

'So,' said Keaton, bringing Harriet's attention back to him. 'Do you like your dress?'

She gazed at her napkin-covered lap. 'Yes. It's nice. Thank you for buying it for me.'

He gave a slight head shake. 'No. It's on loan. Milly will send it back tomorrow.'

'Oh. Erm, okay.'

His fork slowly swirled in some sort of minty pea sauce as he eyed her neckline lustfully. 'This is a nice restaurant. I'm surprised.'

Harriet tried hard not to screw her face up to match her balled fists. 'We have a lot of nice places here.'

Thank you very much.

Keaton gazed around as though silently marking the room out of ten. He smiled warmly at some young lad staring open-mouthed at him, then went back to loved-up mode. He reached for Harriet's hand across the white linen tablecloth and kissed her knuckles.

Harriet was well aware a few phones were sneakily taking pictures of them. Plus, there was Warren, who was outside, peering through the window with his go-go-gadget lens. She smiled politely as Keaton sat back to eat some of his side salad, which was a small pot of cubed cucumber, as specifically requested. And nothing was too much trouble for him. The waitress had made that fact perfectly clear, mostly with fluttering eyelashes.

Yeah, I saw you looking over, Jude Jackson. You were looking straight at my hand being kissed, weren't you? Don't think I don't notice the moments you pay us attention.

Her mind was back at the hotel when Jude had seen her in her dress for the first time. Her acting skills matched Keaton's when she forced her face to remain lifeless when all she wanted to do was grin from ear to ear at the way Jude was looking at her.

Keaton was mimicking the same look Jude had, and the women surrounding them were dreamy-eyed and green-eyed. He was definitely a good actor, and to see him at work was actually quite something for Harriet.

No wonder he earns the big bucks. Shame he's not as nice as he looks. Lexi would call him a rom-protag to look at, but he's not a romance protagonist by personality. They're never shallow or ignorant. Nope, Keaton Byrd definitely wouldn't make it into one of Lexi's romance novels. He's lacking.

Harriet wished she could call Lexi and tell her all about him. She knew her sister would call at some point about the little show. Everyone would.

It didn't take long for an eager fan to make a dash towards Keaton to ask for a selfie. He was about to oblige but Milly was at the table before the woman had time to finish her sentence.

Harriet had never seen anyone look so utterly petrified. The poor woman swallowed hard, her bottom lip quivered, and her legs almost gave way beneath her.

Keaton calmed Milly, smiled warmly at his fan, and handed over her phone to Harriet, asking if she wouldn't mind.

'Erm, no, of course.' Harriet snapped a few shots and handed back the phone.

The woman was ever so pleased. She told Keaton a thousand times over how much she loved his films, and him, of course. Keaton took it all in his stride whilst Milly seemed to telepathically tell the rest of the restaurant they'd better not try their luck.

Harriet leaned closer to him once they were alone again. 'Does that happen a lot when you're eating?'

He bobbed his head and curled his mouth into his famous one-sided smile that melted hearts. 'Happens anywhere.'

'Don't you get fed up?'

'You get used to it.'

Harriet wasn't sure it was something she would want to get used to. She wasn't one to be too bothered about eating in front of people, but when thirty or so were all zooming in on her face, she kind of wished she was invisible.

'Looking forward to hanging by the pool tomorrow?' he asked, waking her from her trance with a twenty-something man licking his lips her way.

'Hmm? Oh, yes. The pool photos. Should be fun. Do you swim much?'

'No. It ruins your skin. All those chemicals. You know.'

'You could try swimming in the sea. Salt water is good for you.'

'I prefer mud baths.'

Harriet lowered her raised eyebrows once she realised how high they were. 'So, I guess that means you don't have a swimming pool back home.'

'I have two. Indoors and outside. The outdoor one has an old-fashioned movie camera on the bottom. Obviously, I don't mean a real one. I'm talking about a picture of one made from tiles. It's pretty cool. You should come out sometime, then you can see it for yourself. Or google my name. It shows up now and again. Aerial view. Not that they had my permission.'

She watched him sip his vodka and caught a trace of vulnerability in his eyes. It soon disappeared, and he was back to smouldering and dreamy face. It didn't take her long to figure out he only had about three expressions. But each one held many depths. She wondered if that was him or a whole heap of acting lessons.

'Did you always want to be an actor?'

'Nope. I wanted to be a rock star. I play guitar and I can sing, but my band was going nowhere fast, and a friend of mine was looking for some extras for a movie he was working on. They were paying, so it seemed a good move.' He paused. 'Don't you know my story?'

Why would I know your story?

She shook her head, trying to give off polite vibes. 'No, sorry.'

He shrugged off her lack of Wikipedia knowledge about his life. 'Well, I ended up with a small role in this movie, and I got asked if I wanted a bigger part in the guy's next gig. There was more money offered. Not a lot back then, but more than I had in my pocket at the time, so I said yes. It was that movie that got me noticed by, they call them *the right people*. My next job was the one that made me famous.

Suddenly, I'm a superstar and everyone wants a piece of me.'

'It must have been quite surreal.'

He smiled to himself, deep in thought. 'Yeah, I guess it was.'

'Your parents must have been proud.'

Keaton sniffed, took a swig of his drink, and held one hand in the air for a split second, which summoned Milly. 'We're leaving. Pay for this lot.'

Milly followed orders as Keaton stood. Jude was instantly by his side, and Harriet guessed she should stand too.

'Everything okay?' whispered Jude to Harriet, as Keaton marched off, giving the occasional obligatory nod to a fan.

'I think so.' She kept her voice low as he escorted her outside. 'I mentioned his parents, and his face dropped.'

Jude shook his head a touch and gave her a warning look as he opened the car door for her.

Harriet took the hint.

Parents off limits.

7

Jude

The swimming pool photoshoot took place in a rented house that had its own private pool. Milly wasn't keen on using the one at Hotel Royale. There were far too many people lurking around hoping to catch a glimpse of the famous film star. Word had seriously got out since the first photo release of Keaton on the Isle of Wight with an unknown woman.

Harriet looked uncomfortable with being made-up for a swim. He could hear her telling Milly nobody swam with a full face of makeup. Milly simply told her they did back home.

The large white towel wrapped around Harriet's body was hiding the skimpy red-and-white polka dot bikini she had been assigned. It was clear Harriet hated the swimwear, especially since she had practically shouted at Milly, 'I'm not wearing that.'

Jude wasn't quite sure how Milly had managed to persuade Harriet to finally put it on, but she did.

Keaton was oblivious to all the hustle and bustle going on around the large rectangular pool. He stayed seated in a comfy black lounger whilst Warren fussed with lighting and a wide cream parasol. The only time Keaton spoke was when his glass of vodka was replaced with a fancy pink cocktail, which did little to amuse or please him in any way.

Jude double-checked the security around the huge contemporary style home. It wasn't fans he was worried about. It was the press. The local reporters were following them everywhere now, but he was on the lookout for the international press. He knew many of them by first name, but they weren't his friends. They were well known for their ruthlessness and brute force at times, not to mention the fact they would pay large sums of money to the paparazzi who got the best shot revealing the latest high-profile couple. That kind of gossip was worth a fortune, and anything to do with Keaton Byrd was front-page news at the moment, thanks to his recent antics.

Jude checked over the side gate. There was no one about, which brought out a deep sigh of relief. He was missing the amount of security they would normally hire back home. Milly's idea of a small circle only put extra pressure on him. He wasn't used to having so many roles at once.

A seagull cried high in the sky, causing Jude's mind to drift back to the sea.

I wonder if I could switch jobs. Get away from all this. Start over. It's not like it's impossible. I have enough savings. I have the know-how. It would probably surprise a few people, except maybe my parents. They know how much I love the ocean. Perhaps I'll make a few calls. Work out some figures. Yeah, it's worth a look, at least.

His eyes nearly popped out of his head as he walked around the corner of the house at the same moment Harriet dropped her towel and wandered over to the side of the pool.

Warren was busy snapping shots whilst ignoring Milly's constant interference, and Keaton had suddenly lost all interest in alcohol.

Jude managed to bring his gaping mouth to a tight close as he struggled to look away from Harriet's amazing figure. She may have hated the swimwear, but he happened to think her athletic body wore it extremely well.

Harriet blushed through her makeup and got told to relax by Warren, who was waving Milly away from leaning over his shoulder.

Jude's attention turned to Keaton as soon as Harriet glanced his way. Embarrassment hit him for getting caught staring at her, even though everyone there was watching her. She was the main attraction at that moment, after all.

Keaton was sitting up straighter, showing concentration and a look Jude had seen many times before.

Oh no, he likes her. He'll make a move on her now. Probably tonight at dinner. Will she fall for his charm? His status? His money? They all do. Why would she be any different? He's Keaton fricking Byrd, for crying out loud. And it's none of my business what Harriet does.

He could feel cracks appear inside his heart, and he knew it was because he also liked Harriet, and he didn't want her to fall in love with his boss.

A million words flowed through his mind, causing arguments, problems, and unnecessary drama. His made-up scenarios were causing his chest to tighten and his head to ache. He had to take a breath and regain some control, because he was getting ahead of himself.

Harriet won't fall for him. He's not her type. Not sure whose type he is, but he's definitely not hers. There is no way in a zillion years he would live here, and she wouldn't want to live anywhere else. Yeah, he is out of luck with this one. But what if she's happy for a summer fling with him? Something short and memorable.

He rolled his eyes at himself.

Like this wouldn't be memorable as it is. Jeez, Jude, get a grip. She's not your girl. You can't think outside the box with this one. She's here for Keaton. Doing what we're paying her to do. This is for her future with her son. It doesn't involve you. Argh!

He had to stay professional. Get the job done. Go home. Figure out his life. He wanted to be like her. Do the things that made him smile. Be happy.

She's happy. Although, she's not showing that right now.

He glanced over to see another minor dispute taking place between Harriet and Milly. Approaching them, he intervened. 'What's the problem?'

Harriet met his gaze, causing a thump to his heart. She wrapped her arms around her chest, and Jude could tell she felt exposed in the bikini, even more so in front of him, it would appear.

He reached back to a lounger and handed her the white towel, thinking a conversation whilst she was covered up was in everyone's best interest. Well, mainly his, because he couldn't concentrate.

As though reading his mind, a hint of a smile hit the corner of Harriet's mouth as she wrapped the towel around her body, tucking its soft fibres under her arms.

Milly huffed, and her hands flapped to her hips. 'She's being her usual awkward self, Jude.'

Harriet's raised eyebrows only showed her amazement at Milly's statement. She turned back to Jude and pointed at the poolside. 'She wants me to stretch out like some sort of sex symbol.'

Jude swallowed hard at the thought.

Milly scowled at her. 'What's wrong with that?'

Harriet's fingers dug deeper into her towel, turning her knuckles white. 'I'm not a model.'

Milly scoffed. 'No. A model would get on with it.'

Harriet glared at her for a moment and then turned back to Jude for his help. 'I'm not doing it.'

He asked Milly to give them a moment, and she happily obliged, heading over to see if Keaton needed anything.

Jude slowly looked all the way up Harriet's towel to finally settle at her eyes, open wide with amusement. He swallowed, went to speak, held back, cleared his throat, and pulled himself together. 'Harriet, you don't have to do anything you're not comfortable with. Warren will take whatever photos you're happy to do. Milly has no power over you, no matter what she thinks. Ignore her. I'll have a word. Is there anything else you'd like to discuss with me?'

And that's how it's done. Very professional, Jude. Pat yourself on the back. You've got this.

Her beauty that reminded him of the ocean was all too much.

Okay, you can move, Jude. There are other things to look at.

He tried to hold back a smile as his attention moved to her faint freckles he secretly adored.

'How much longer are we going to be here, Jude?' Her voice was soft, making him instantly concerned.

She looks sad. I'll wrap this up.

'Let me talk to Warren. I'm guessing he'll want some shots of you and Keaton sitting together. Something more natural than what Milly had in mind. Will that be okay?'

She lowered her head and gave a slight nod. 'I feel stupid.'

'Well, you don't look it, Hal. You look amazing, but I understand.'

She reached forward and gently nudged his bare forearm before going back to clutching her towel. That one simple touch released a fizz into his stomach and a small amount of oxygen to leave his whirling brain.

56

'Thanks, Jude. Sometimes I think you're the only one here who does.'

'It'll all be over soon, Harriet. Only a few more public shows of affection over the next couple of weeks, and we'll be gone from your life.'

Her eyes almost sparkled, and he wasn't sure if it was from the strong sunlight bouncing off the water or if he had simply imagined the look.

'You're the only one I'd miss, Jude.'

It wasn't her words. It was the way she said them. Soft, gentle, filled with meaning and something he couldn't quite put his finger on, or rather, something he was afraid to confirm to himself.

She took a step closer towards him, so much so, he could smell the tropical sun cream on her skin. 'In case I'm not making myself clear. I like hanging out with you.'

Milly's loud voice ordering everyone, except Keaton, back to work shattered the moment building between Jude and Harriet. He wanted to say something back to her, but now Warren was by his side, and Harriet was being ushered over to the lounger to sit by Keaton.

Was that her way of telling me she likes me? Really likes me?

8

Harriet

Good grief, I can't believe we had to leave the restaurant early because of the growing crowd outside. How on earth does Keaton feel safe when his life is so chaotic like that?

Harriet's heart was still racing, and she was hungry. She'd only got through a starter when Sergeant Milly took over and herded them back to the hotel.

Why would anyone want this for their life? I'll be glad when this is over. I still can't believe strangers know my name. They were calling me, asking me questions. My phone hasn't stopped ringing. Mum's going to be fuming if reporters show up at our house.

She was so thankful Tommy was at a sleepover. At least she knew he was out of harm's way. She looked out the window of Keaton's suite, knowing the view was of the sea.

Wish I could swim far away from this madness.

She turned to see Keaton and his vodka, and Milly and her electronic notebook. Jude had disappeared, and Harriet wished she could too.

Keaton poured her an unwanted drink and patted the sofa, gesturing for her to sit by his side. 'You good?' he asked quietly, as though his throat were sore or he couldn't actually be bothered to speak at all.

Harriet slumped, almost tempted to take the alcohol and down the lot. 'It's all a bit much, isn't it?'

He raised his eyebrows and nodded into his glass. 'You think you could get used to it?'

'No thanks. You can keep that life.'

Keaton tapped her knee. 'You could come back to mine, hang out for a while with me, learn how to cope with my life.' He grinned wickedly. 'Share my bed for real.'

Harriet laughed. She didn't mean to. It just came bursting out. 'You're very forward, aren't you?'

'Don't see the point in wasting time, Hadley. So, what do you say? You want in?'

She was still laughing at his choice of words whilst Milly edged away, trying to make herself disappear into the background. 'Want in? That's how you ask out a woman?'

He shrugged and flashed her his money smile. 'I don't normally have to ask.'

'No, I guess you don't.'

He leaned over and nudged her arm with his own. 'Hey, it's a good opportunity being with me.'

A stab of sadness hit her. She studied his face whilst he immersed it into his vodka. There was something so vulnerable about him when he was out of the public eye. Something resembling lonely. She wondered if anyone had ever truly loved him. Did he know love? Jude had told her in private that Keaton's parents gave him a crappy childhood. One filled with alcohol and chaos. No wonder he was so used to that kind of life. She had to ask. 'Have you ever been in love, Keaton?'

He lowered his glass at the same time Milly left the room. Leaning back into the softness of the sofa, he gazed dreamily over to the far wall at a painting of the shops in the small bay next door to Sandly.

'Juliette Lock.' His chest lifted and fell steadily as he smiled a smile that seem to be just for him.

'When was that?'

'Oh, back when I was seventeen.' He flapped one hand in the air. 'Before all this. She was my high school sweetheart. You know, I came from a small town too.'

Harriet nodded. She was enjoying the relaxed version of Keaton happily being revealed to her. 'What was she like?'

'Beautiful.' His smile widened. 'In every way. She was always a good girl. Helpful, happy, caring, cute. I never understood what she saw in me.' He turned to face Harriet. 'My family was a lot poorer than hers back then. I didn't have the best clothes or a nice car. But she liked me. You know, she came on to me. I was kind of shy back then. Yeah, I know, it's hard to believe.'

They both laughed, and Harriet settled back, waiting to hear more about Keaton's past.

'She was actually my first kiss, and everything else. Some of the more popular kids used to tease her because she was with me, but she never gave in to them. I wanted to fight them all the time, especially this one guy, who I know was jealous. But Juliette would ignore them and kiss me even harder on those bad days.' He stilled for a moment, losing his smile. 'She was something else.'

'What happened in the end? Why did you break up?'

He scoffed and shook his head a touch as though scolding himself. 'I got famous.'

'She didn't like that?'

'I had already left town, with the promise of returning after she had finished medical school. I never did.'

Harriet's eyes widened in surprise. 'Never?'

Keaton swigged his drink and pursed his lips for a moment. 'I used to visit her where she was studying to become a nurse. We were still close then. When my life started to change, I called her. Asked her to join me, but I'd been gone for a while by then, and I think she stopped believing in me. God knows I did.'

'Oh.' Harriet placed her hand over her heart as though it was hers breaking.

That's so sad.

A sudden thought hit her hard, causing frown lines and folded arms. 'Why didn't you fight for her? She fought for you all through high school, and she stayed with you even when she was away studying.'

Keaton opened his mouth to speak but then closed it again as though at a loss for words.

Harriet tapped his foot with her own. 'Keaton, you should have fought hard. Have you ever loved anyone as much as her since?'

I already know you'll say no. I know she's your one and only. Oh goodness, this is pure romance stuff. I want him to have his happy ending, like he does in some of his films. He's such a stupid idiot.

'She's actually the only person I've loved. Ever. I didn't even love my family.'

'Then, why let her go? You make no sense.'

Keaton scoffed into his vodka. 'Nothing about my life makes sense. Do you know how much money people pay me for acting? Just acting, nothing else. That's all I do. I don't save lives or invent world-changing things. I don't even do my own stunts. I stand in front of a camera and pretend to be someone else, like you're doing for me. People want to be me. Be near me. They think they know me. And they want a piece of that. It's all a bunch of crap. Why do you think I'm on my own? No one stays around me for long. Not once they see a real flawed human being. It's not the dream they had in mind.'

Harriet held his hand. 'I'm sorry, Keaton. I guess nobody thinks about that.'

'Nope. It's all moonlight and roses. Juliette knew me. She took the time.' He twiddled with the hem of his top. 'I broke her heart. I was so swept away by all the limelight, I couldn't see what was real anymore. When I look back, I see us in a storm, and she's blown one way, and I'm stranded on some weird island.' He laughed out loud. 'Bit like now.'

'Hey.' Harriet tapped his knuckles before pulling her hand back to her lap. 'The Isle of Wight isn't weird.'

'Nah, you're right. It's kind of cute, I guess.'

'What was your home like?'

'You ever seen the movie *Footloose*?'

She smiled as she nodded. 'Like that?'

'Pretty much, but without all the dancing.'

Harriet shared her thoughts out loud. 'I wonder if Juliette still lives there?'

'She does.'

Her head whipped around to face him full on, catching the twinkle in his smile. 'You know?'

Keaton held his hands up, showing his palms. 'Okay, don't judge me, but I keep track of her.'

'Wow, like a stalker.'

He laughed as her smile widened. 'No. I just... I don't know. Do you think I'm weird?'

'What, weirder than I already thought? Hmm, let me see. Well...' She tried for serious. 'I think you never stopped loving her, and you regret not going home.'

Keaton twisted his lips, holding back his smile. 'Oh, really? That's what you got from spending five minutes with me?'

'Tell me I'm wrong, and I'll shut up.'

Blimming heck, you can't. You still love her. I wonder if she feels the same way. Wouldn't it be romantic. She's probably what he needs to sort his head out. He needs love. Real, unconditional, true love.

Keaton brushed his hand over his beard and sighed, lowering his drink to the coffee table. 'Ah, it was a long time ago now. Life moves on. People move on.'

'Well, that's up to you, isn't it? You know something, Keaton Byrd, you're not much of a fighter.'

'Oh, is that right?'

'You hate your life, and yet, you do little to change it. You still love someone, but you won't fight for her. You just waste away, drinking and working.'

'Well, thank you, Miss Therapist.'

Harriet softened her voice. 'Keaton, why don't you move your chess piece? It's your turn. That's what my dad says.'

'Maybe because I'm not interested in playing the game.'

'But are you interested in seeing what's down the left lane? You've been walking down the right lane for so long now, isn't it worth a peek? For curiosity? One tiny, minuscule, itsy-bitsy look. Might actually be something exciting going on over there. Look at me, I'm trying something new. Radical, even.'

Keaton turned, amusement filling his face. 'What you got in mind?'

'Juliette. What's her life like, Mr Stalker?'

He chewed his bottom lip as he breathed out a sharp laugh.

Harriet goaded him. 'Come on, we both know you have details.'

'Okay.' He shook his head and relaxed. 'She's a nurse at the hospital out of town to where we grew up, and she also does some home visits to the elderly. That's her department.

She has a younger half-sister, who she lived with, and who has gone away to college. So, she lives alone at the moment. She's thirty-nine, same as me, and she's single. She's always led a pretty quiet life. Sometimes, I've worried about her over the years. I want her to be happy. To have love and a family.'

'She might still be happy. Some people are happy on their own. Maybe her work makes her happy.'

'She always loved helping others. She's not a selfish jerk like me.'

Harriet moved his glass away as he reached for his drink. 'You would be so different if you were happy, Keaton. But you choose to be hard on yourself.'

He frowned at her hand clasped around his vodka. 'You're too young to be this wise.'

He can't go on like this. Uncaring. Playing up to his alter ego. Looking for answers in all the wrong places. She could be exactly what he needs to turn his drunken mess of a life around.

'Hey, why don't we contact her?'

Even the shock of that statement failed to move Keaton from his laid-back posture and persona. 'You think I should contact Juliette? Just like that? Out of the blue?'

Harriet gave a half-shrug. 'Why not? What's the worst that can happen?' He went to answer, but she got in first. 'Forget that part. Look, you're both single, you still love her, you obviously can't get her out of your head, so why not reach out to see how the land lies. Make a move, Movie Man.'

He sat up straighter, suddenly looking keen. 'And say what?'

'Hello.'

'Yeah, we're gonna need more than that.'

'Do you have her number?'

'Why would I have her number?'

Harriet giggled into her hand. 'Please. You so have her number, don't you?'

'Okay, so I might. But it would seem weird to send her a text. She'd know I must have asked around to get her private info.'

'No, you would never do that. PI, yes?'

'Will you stop judging me?'

'Okay, but we need to start somewhere. Your life is in tatters, and I really believe love will save your bleak soul.'

He raised his eyebrows in amusement. 'Bleak soul?'

Harriet ignored him. 'What about an email? That might seem less intrusive. Plus, you can write more.'

'It would still seem odd for me to have access to that.'

'Ooh, Facebook, Instagram. Has she joined anything?'

'She's on Facebook, but she doesn't post much. Just charity events the hospital run. Stuff like that.'

'Wow, you even stalked her there.'

Keaton tossed a cushion at her lap.

Harriet threw it to one side and jumped up to get his laptop from the side table. 'Show me her page.'

Keaton scoffed, trying not to laugh. 'I'm not showing you her page.'

'Oh, come on. I want to see what the love of your life looks like.'

'She is not the love of my—'

Harriet cleared her throat dramatically. 'Really? You were actually going to finish that sentence?'

'Give me that.' He snatched the laptop and fired it up whilst grimacing and half-smiling in between.

Harriet clapped in front of her chest, earning her a disbelieving shake of the head from Keaton.

'I can't believe I'm doing this,' he huffed out quietly.

Harriet sat on her heels and snuggled into his side, patiently watching the screen.

He glanced at her face. 'You comfy?'

She smiled and nodded at the laptop. 'This is so exciting.'

'No, it's not. It's nerve-racking.'

Harriet gasped with delight as Juliette's profile picture came into view. 'Ooh, she's pretty, Keaton. She has a country-girl look.' She could see him out of her peripheral vision frowning her way. 'You know, homely, fresh face, down to earth. That type.'

'She was that type.'

'How long did your relationship with her last in total?'

'Around four years.' He sighed deeply. 'Best four years of my life.'

Harriet watched him look thoughtfully at Juliette's face. A wide smile, green eyes, and blonde curls brought the photo to life for him.

He shook his head, giving the impression he was talking to himself. 'Time sure does fly.'

'Hmm. So, let's not waste any more. Go into her message box. You need to write something.'

It was the first time she had seen Keaton look utterly lost. His mouth gaped slightly as his eyes narrowed at the screen. 'What the hell am I supposed to say?'

Harriet was thinking just as hard as him.

What would you say to an old love you haven't spoken to in years? Hello just doesn't cut it. Come on, Hal. Think. He needs help here.

'Well, perhaps you could start by saying hi.'

Keaton typed in the word, then glanced her way.

Harriet focused on the screen. 'Erm. I was just thinking about you—'

'Nope. I'm not saying that.'

She tilted her head to one side and grinned. 'I thought you were the straightforward type. You're not shy. Be you.'

'I am being me. This is me. She knows the real me. Inside and out. I don't care how long we've been apart. She still knows the real me. And I'm not confident around her.'

'But you're older now. She will have grown as a person too. You can use everything you have learned over the years to communicate with her now. Draw on your experience.'

'My experience tells me to act, but it's lying. It's not showing the real me.'

'Isn't there a saying about dressing for the role you want instead of the one you have?'

Keaton shook his head whilst staring at the flashing cursor. 'I don't want to act. I want to say hi.'

'Well, we've got that far. Okay, why don't you say exactly that. I just wanted to say hi.'

He typed out the words, and they both took a moment to read over the small amount they had come up with so far.

Harriet tapped the laptop. 'Change hi to *Hey, Juliette.*'

He did as instructed and smiled at the result. 'Okay, that's a good start. Now what?'

Harriet scrunched her hands together in front of her chest. 'Ooh, how about, I was wondering if you would like to meet up for coffee one day.'

'Coffee?'

She glanced at his glass of vodka sitting on the table. 'I don't think you should take her to a bar.'

He sniffed and twisted his lips. 'Coffee seems formal.'

'There is nothing formal about coffee.'

'Yeah, but it raises questions.'

Now she was confused. 'What questions?'

'Are we meeting for a catch-up or does it sound as if I'm asking for a date. And does coffee even mean coffee these days, because I can't keep up with all the hidden meanings anymore.'

'Okay, point taken. So, how about we clarify by saying something like… I was wondering if you would like to meet up one day for a coffee so we can catch up. It would be good to see you again.'

Keaton raised a ringed index finger in the air. 'Yes. I like that.' He typed out her words and smiled to himself.

Harriet scrunched her nose. 'We could add a little lie to make it sound better.'

'What kind of lie?' He already looked far from keen on the idea of lying to Juliette.

'You could say you were going to be in town for a while—'

'Why would I be in town?'

Harriet huffed at his snap. She folded her arms and tightened her brow. 'Well, why not go home? It's a great excuse to see her. You could do some sort of hospital visit famous people do. Donate money to the place where you grew up. Maybe the church needs a new roof, or the school library needs more books. Plus, you could do with putting some demons to bed, and it seems to me your hometown is where all your troubles started. Sometimes, your past has to be dealt with.'

'The thought of going back there raises anxiety levels in me and a need for more than that bottle of vodka.'

'Fair enough, but what does the thought of never seeing Juliette again do to you?'

'I've made it work up until you came along.'

Harriet smiled and patted his arm. 'Keaton, I don't think things have worked for you for a long time. Press send. Fight for her. Go home and face your fears. Face Juliette. Apologise. It's a start. Even if you two can't rekindle anything, at least you would have put all those regrets and doubts to bed that you have swirling around in your head.'

'Are you trying to say I need closure?'

Harriet smiled warmly, hoping he would see the help she was trying to give. It didn't seem many had tried so hard with him before. He certainly didn't seem used to that sort of care and attention. 'I don't know. Maybe.'

Keaton sent the message and inhaled deeply. He closed the laptop and turned her way. 'Your turn.'

Harriet shook her head slightly and furrowed her brow. 'What do you mean, my turn?'

A wash of glee filled his face, revealing his charm and boyish look. 'You think I don't see the way you check out my PA?'

'Jude?'

'He's in the room below me.'

'I know which room he's in. I work here, remember?'

Keaton gestured towards the door. 'Don't mind me.'

'There's nothing going on with me and Jude.'

'Probably because you're sitting here with me.'

Harriet snorted out a laugh.

'Hey,' said Keaton, grinning widely. 'He looks at you the same way. So, how about you go do some fighting of your own. And after what you just made me do, I'm thinking this is some sort of payback.'

'Are you actually telling me to go hit on your personal assistant?'

'I'm advising you to go take a peek at what's going on over there in his lane.'

Harriet couldn't help but laugh as she glanced over at the door.

Could I? Should I?

9

Jude

Jude opened his hotel door to see Harriet standing there looking somewhat awkward and unsure. He was just as unsure. It was getting late, and he thought she'd gone home. Although his mind had repeatedly told him she was upstairs, lying in the arms of Keaton Byrd. Oh, how those thoughts had plagued him for the last couple of hours.

The fake romantic dinner had gone awry, and all the fuss had caused a headache. Without anyone noticing, he had slipped away to curl up on his bed and sulk the night away. Now he had to face the one person he was trying to avoid.

He peered over her shoulder to see the corridor was empty. 'Harriet, is something wrong?'

'Can I come in?' she asked sweetly.

Jude pulled the door wider, allowing entrance automatically before he had time to process her being in his room and think better of the situation. 'Can I get you a drink, Hal?'

She sat on the chair by the window and shook her head. 'No, ta. I'm good.'

His room wasn't a suite like Keaton's. There was a double bed and a small table with two chairs. A dresser took up one wall and an internal door led to a bathroom. He sat on the edge of his messy bed, scanning his floor for signs of underwear, which he knew wouldn't be there but still felt the need to check.

'Everything okay, Harriet? I thought you'd gone home.'

'Aren't you supposed to chauffeur me?'

He jumped up immediately. 'Oh, sorry. I'm not used to doing the driving. I forgot.'

She broke out into a huge smile and laughed whilst waving at him to sit. 'I'm kidding.'

He plopped himself back down. 'You might be, but it is what I'm supposed to do. Especially now the reporters are lurking. You can't go home alone.'

'I've been walking around these streets alone since I was a kid.'

'Things are different now, Hal. Those people are relentless. They will only hound you all the way to your door. I'll drive you as soon as you're ready.' He shot her a quizzical look. 'Erm, is that the only reason you're here?'

Harriet's cheeks flushed, and her eyes weren't meeting his. Her feet began to fidget, and her fingers on her right hand clamped over the ones on her left.

Jude could feel all her tension, and it was starting to make him nervous. He brushed his hand around the back of his neck, thinking about what else he could say, as she was clearly struggling with words. He hoped Keaton hadn't done anything to upset her.

Perhaps she wants out of this stupid contract. I don't blame her. This whole thing is bizarre, and we've got horse riding tomorrow. Oh, she might be worried about that. She probably can't ride.

He went to ask about the horse riding, but she got up from the chair and sat by his side on the bed, taking all words from his mouth and head for a moment. He swallowed hard, knowing full well his Adam's apple was bobbing up and down as though it had been tossed out into the ocean during a windy day.

Harriet still hadn't spoken, but it looked as though she had something to say.

He had to ask. 'Is this about the horse riding tomorrow, Hal? Are you worried? You don't have to—'

Harriet propelled herself forward, placing her lips straight onto his, silencing him.

Oh my God.

Jude stilled on her mouth. She wasn't moving, and he needed a moment for his brain to receive the memo.

After what seemed like a lifetime, Harriet went to pull away, but Jude had come back to life. He placed his hand on the back of her head and pulled her back to his mouth, where he kissed her with more passion than he'd ever mustered. He even surprised himself.

Everything about the kiss was perfect to him. The warmth from her mouth. Her gentle tongue trying to match the moves he found hard to control. And when her arms wrapped around him, he was lost in her.

Harriet tugged at his tee-shirt, letting him know she wanted it off.

He obliged and then stilled as she pulled away from his mouth and placed one hand tenderly over his heart. Her fingertips lightly brushed down his chest, causing a wave of adrenaline to flood him completely. He placed his hand over hers as she reached for the rim of his pyjama bottoms. 'Hal. Are you sure?'

She took a breath and met his eyes. 'Jude, I really like you, and I haven't had feelings for anyone since Tommy's father. I'm sorry if I'm rushing this. I don't mean to. I was talking with Keaton about love, and, well, I guess it all went to my head. The next thing I know, I'm knocking on your door.' She lowered her gaze. 'I don't know what I'm doing, Jude. I just know I like you. A lot.'

Her soft tone and sweet manner went straight to his heart. He couldn't help smiling into the top of her bowed head.

'I like you a lot too, Harriet.' He kissed her hair and leaned back, lifting her chin.

She blushed and let out the smallest of laughs whilst covering her face with one hand.

'Hey.' Jude carefully removed her fingers from her cheeks and lightly kissed each one. 'If it's any consolation, I don't know what I'm doing either. We could figure it out together, if you like.'

She nodded into his chest, then hugged him, curling up onto his lap.

Jude held her close and kissed her head, then laughed quietly into her dark hair. 'This wasn't how I saw my night ending.'

'Me neither.'

He swirled his hand around on her back, not knowing what to do next.

I think she needs more time with me. I don't want her having any regrets about moving too fast. It's her decision. I have to ask.

'Hal, do you want to stay the night?'

She sat up and looked at him. Their faces inches apart. She lightly brushed her lips over his, causing all his butterflies to launch straight into his solar plexus. 'I do, Jude. And I can, as Tommy's at a sleepover, but…' She paused.

Okay, I get it. You want to take it slow. That's cool. I've got this. I've got her. She has nothing to worry about. I need to make sure she knows that.

'Harriet, I wanna wake up with you by my side. We can just share a bed. I'll hold you all night. You want that? Do you wanna slow things down?'

She nodded. 'Yes. Will you be comfortable with that?'

He breathed out a laugh filled with confusion. 'Of course. Why wouldn't I be? Hal, we've just met. We're still getting to know each other. I don't expect anything from you, and I sure as hell don't want you to do anything you don't feel one hundred percent comfortable with. You're in control here, okay? You call the shots. I'm ready when you are.'

She kissed him, running her hands through his sun-kissed hair, and Jude knew he was going to have a hard time holding back, but he had given his word, and he meant everything he said. There was no way he would make her feel she needed to give more than she was ready for. Even if she was lying naked by his side, he wouldn't want her to feel obligated to have sex with him.

He suddenly remembered the birds and the bees talk his mother had given him back when he was sixteen, only none of it was about the actual act of sex, just respect. She had sat him down and explained exactly what the word *no* meant, told him about equality in a relationship, and not to make assumptions or have expectations. That day, Sara Jackson made sure her son knew how to be a gentleman, a man without entitlement, and above all else a decent human being.

He pulled back and smiled, nudging Harriet's nose with his own. 'You're so beautiful, Hal. Why do you wanna be with a guy like me?'

She squashed her mouth onto his cheek and breathed out a laugh. 'I think I'm the one punching above my weight here.'

'Erm, no, you're not.' He tucked her hair behind her ear and kissed her cheek. 'I need to get you out of your clothes and into one of my tees.'

'Is that what I'm sleeping in?'

'If you like.'

Harriet's face was practically glowing from her smile. 'Ooh, I like very much.'

75

Jude gestured at the television on the dresser. 'We could watch a movie in bed. I have snacks, and the little kettle over there is dying to be boiled so we can make hot chocolate.' He scrunched his nose at the small sachets sitting in a white bowl on a tray beside the kettle. 'I had one last night. It's not the best but it's okay.'

Harriet followed his eyes to the dresser. The deep sigh leaving her didn't go unnoticed.

He hugged her closer, resting his lips by her warm ear. 'Hey, you don't have to have a sleepover with me. It's cool. I can drive you home whenever you're ready.'

She tightened her hold on him. 'I want to stay with you all night, Jude.'

Her words rendered him useless for a few minutes. The fact she pushed him backwards onto the bed and was kissing him deeply wasn't helping his brain much.

'You take my clothes off, Jude, and put one of your tops on me. I want you to. Just leave my knickers on.'

Wake up, Jude. Get a grip. She wants something from you. Get with the system. Come on. Do what she asks.

He slowly undressed her, taking his time to scan her toned muscles, stopping every few seconds to kiss her body, and pulling back for air each time she took his breath with her lips, he finally got her out of her clothes and into his surfboard print tee-shirt.

Harriet snuggled in his bed whilst he made their hot drinks.

He couldn't help peering over his shoulder at her and only stopped to concentrate on his task when he burned his finger on the spout of the kettle.

There was something so calming about sitting up in bed with her. He felt relaxed as though they had shared that moment many times before.

They laughed when he switched on the TV to discover the hotel had programmed in a whole heap of Keaton Byrd films.

'I'm not watching him.' Jude turned the channel and settled on *Roman Holiday*.

Harriet snuggled up to him and started to kiss all over his face again, making him laugh.

'I thought we were going to watch a movie.'

'We can, but we can also kiss, and then kiss some more.'

He pulled her further into the plump pillows. 'Yeah, I like the kissing part.'

Harriet rolled on top of his chest, pinning him to the bed, and as he kind of liked it, he let her take charge. Her mouth trailed his neck, chest, and stomach, and he was sure he might happily die that way. 'Is this okay, Jude? Just kissing?'

He stroked back her hair and dipped her head so he could kiss the bridge of her nose, knowing full well he was about to pepper kisses over each and every adorable freckle. 'Yeah, Hal. It's perfect.'

10

Harriet

Lucky Riding Stables was having one of its quarterly events, where it opened to a minibus of kids from an underprivileged area for the day. Primary school children were riding, mucking out, grooming the horses, and being farmhands in the warm sunshine; all of which did little to spark joy in Milly, who was worried she might catch a stomach bug, or worse, she'd told Harriet as soon as she spotted the twelve children mooching around.

Jude opened the car door for everyone to step out onto the driveway in front of the small farmhouse. 'They're kids, Milly. Jeez.'

Harriet muffled her laugh.

I don't think Milly was ever a child. I can't imagine her playing with leaves or jumping off a roundabout while it's spinning.

Harriet waved at the owner of the stables as she approached. 'Hello, Rhett. These are the Americans I was telling you about, but no doubt you've already heard Keaton Byrd was here.' She gestured at an intrigued Keaton, who was giving Rhett the once over. 'Everyone, this is Rhett Smithson, owner of Lucky Riding Stables.'

Milly scrunched her nose as Jude stepped forward to shake Rhett's outstretched hand.

Rhett eyed them all, her hazel irises holding the slightest of twinkles. 'Yeah, I've heard all about the famous film star coming to town.' She nodded towards Keaton and flashed him a wide smile. 'Can you really ride, or do you have stuntman for the job?'

Keaton raised his eyebrows as he closed in on the front porch. 'Me? I can ride. I had to learn a few years back for a role, which came in handy later in a couple of other movies. I like to think I'm pretty good at it now.'

Rhett folded her slightly muscular arms and pulled in her bottom lip. 'Hmm, we'll see.'

Keaton rolled out a hand and almost bowed. 'Show me to your stables, Miss Smithson.'

'Come on then.' Rhett guided them around the back of her house, to the stables.

Harriet felt Jude tug her back slightly so they were walking behind everyone else. She glanced his way, and he winked, then playfully nudged her arm with his own. 'Stop, Jude,' she whispered, desperately wanting to pull his face closer and kiss his lips. 'No PDAs, remember?'

He tipped his head so he was near her ear. 'I can't help it. I want to put my arm around you.' He gestured to the stables as they approached. 'Hey, I bet we can find somewhere in there to make out.'

Harriet snorted out a quiet laugh and slapped her hand over her mouth. 'We'll end up smelling like manure.'

'I can live with that.' He reached out and quickly tickled her ribs, causing her to squirm away.

Milly turned sharply to them, and they moved apart as though the other was made of fire. 'Will you two hurry up?' She flapped one hand whilst using the other to hold a tissue to her nose. 'This place smells worse than the donkeys,' she mumbled, mainly to herself.

Harriet had to move away from Jude before she found herself leaping into his arms. Spending the night in that exact place had only made her want to hold on to him even more than she did before. Waking up next to Jude was one of the best feelings she'd ever had. The only downside was she had to get up, go home, get changed, and then go out for the day with him, pretending she didn't adore him so completely.

Keaton turned away from talking to Rhett to face Harriet. 'Did you know her name comes from *Gone with the Wind*? Her parents were fans of the movie.'

Harriet nodded. 'Yeah, and her sister's called Vivien.'

'Is she as pretty?'

Harriet nudged him and shook her head. She leaned in closer so she could whisper in his ear. 'Any word on Juliette yet?'

He twisted his mouth to one side and shook his head slightly.

'Oh, well, never mind, Keaton. It's early days.' She caught Jude looking over. His brow was tight, and his lips pursed.

He doesn't look too pleased about something. Oh, it's because I'm so close to Keaton's face. Jude's jealous. Well, well, what do you know. It would appear he likes me as much as I like him. Wow, could I have found someone to be with? I'd do a cartwheel if it weren't for the fact he'll go back to his own country soon, and I'll never see him again. Oh, why did I have to fall for him?

Keaton's nose was suddenly pressed against her cheek, making their interaction look cosy and sweet. 'I haven't had a drink since you made me send that message, you know. I'm feeling a bit queasy.'

'Is that your excuse for not getting on a horse? Did you lie to Rhett about your riding skills? Hmm. I'm thinking you are a bit of a chicken, Keaton Byrd.'

He pulled back, full of amusement. 'I can ride. You'll see in a minute. It's you we should be worried about. Been on a horse before?'

Harriet shrugged and glanced at Jude to see he was petting a dapple grey over by the entrance. 'When I was a kid. I'll be okay. No one's bothered about me anyway. All eyes are on you, as usual.'

A nine-year-old boy came over and handed Keaton a brush. 'Do you want to help groom this one?' he asked casually, pointing at the small brown pony to his side.

Harriet followed the lad inside and watched as Keaton and the kid started to brush the calm pony.

'I haven't done this in a while,' he confessed to the child.

The boy nodded and carried on with his task. 'I like it, and I like riding my bike. The chain broke, but I fixed it. My dad said I wouldn't be able to, but I did. He said I'm no good at anything, but I can do stuff.'

Harriet raised her eyebrows in surprise, but Keaton didn't seem fazed by the lack of encouragement at the child's home. 'I'm sure you're very good at stuff.' She smiled his way and nodded, but the boy carried on brushing the pony.

Ooh, I'm so mad. If anyone ever told my Tommy he wasn't good at anything, I'd lose it, I'm sure. Poor boy. What a thing for his dad to say.

Keaton sniffed and cuffed his nose. 'My dad was like that,' he told the lad. 'But I didn't listen. Do you know why?'

The boy shook his head and waited for the answer.

'Because I taught myself how to play the guitar.' Keaton sniffed again and petted the pony's head. 'No matter what anyone said to me, I would ignore them, then go and play my guitar. I was proving to myself I wasn't worthless, you see. I could do something. Don't forget that about yourself, kid. There is always something you can do.'

'Rhett says that too. This is my third time here. I wish I lived here. Do you like where you live?'

Harriet leaned on the stable door, intrigued to know the answer herself. Even Warren had stopped taking photos.

Keaton shrugged and mumbled something no one heard, then appeared to nod to himself before saying, 'Not really.'

Harriet could only imagine how gorgeous his house was.

I hope Juliette gets in touch. Maybe that's where his home should be. I need to get him to visit the place where he grew up.

She wondered where the kid lived. Bless him, he looked so content. She knew her Tommy was lucky to have happiness and access to his favourite hobby every day.

Lord knows what he would do if he couldn't swim each day.

The children Rhett invited to the stables didn't have many opportunities, and Keaton didn't have the best start either. Harriet wondered if he was thinking about his own childhood.

Jude appeared by her side and peered over at his boss chatting away with the child. He furrowed his eyebrows at Harriet and gently tapped her arm. 'I see he's made a new friend.'

She turned and pushed him further away from prying eyes. 'Jude, will you help me when we have to ride? Walk beside me or something. Have you seen how high these creatures are? I'm a bit nervous.'

Jude glanced over his shoulder, then quickly gave her a peck on the lips. 'You'll be fine. Warren only needs a few shots. I'll stay by your side. Anyway, looks like Keaton might go out riding with the kids instead. Look.'

Harriet turned to see Keaton, the boy, and Rhett leading the pony out to be saddled. She smiled to herself at the scene, then smiled from the inside out when Jude's finger lightly brushed against her own. She met the mischief in his eyes and the grin twitching at the corner of his mouth. Everyone was outside, so she balled his shirt in her fist, tugged him towards the stable, pressed their lips together, and held her breath as his hands cupped her face.

'Harriet,' he mumbled in between kisses. 'I'm taking you home in a minute or down to this straw.'

She giggled and tidied her hair, gesturing for him to leave before her. 'Get outside. Milly will come look for us if we stay in here.'

He waggled his eyebrows as he laughed. 'Won't she get a surprise.'

Harriet nudged him along. 'Come on, let's go find the others.'

He tugged her back, spinning her into his arms, and kissed her neck, making her wriggle. 'I want to stay here with you.'

She stopped his wandering hands and held on to his chin so his mouth would stay still. 'Hey, how about we check out the fish restaurant tonight I was telling you about? You, me, and Tommy. What do you say?'

He took her hand away from his chin and lightly kissed her fingertips. 'I say, it's a date.'

'We'll have to act like we're just hanging out.'

He gave a half-shrug as he headed for outside. 'That's cool.'

Keaton gestured to a rather large dark horse. 'Hey, Harriet, this one's yours.' He grinned, then turned to Milly, and Harriet overheard him tell his assistant to donate a large lump of money to the stables' charity.

That man has a bigger heart than he shows the world. That's it. I'm on a mission. I'm going to make sure by the time he leaves the Isle of Wight, he has direction, meaning, and a mission of his own. To find love. Real love. Meanwhile, I'm going to have to do something about what is happening between me and Jude. There's no way I want him to go home. He can't leave. I have to figure something out for us. This can't just be a fling.

11

Jude

It was early evening, the sky was still blue, the air warm, and Jude was loving every moment sitting at the dinner table outside the fish restaurant in the small paved area lined with white fairy lights and tubs of colourful flowers. It was hard for him to keep his eyes off Harriet. All he wanted to do was gaze dreamily at her, in her pink summer dress and cream cardigan, her small flat shoes, and light makeup allowing her nose freckles to still be visible. She looked delightful in every way, and there was something about her making him feel calm and at ease with his life.

Tommy was happily munching away on fish fingers whilst sitting sideways so he could stare at the moored boats in Sandly Harbour, and Harriet was enjoying a crab salad and a cold glass of white wine.

She glanced up from her plate, and Jude's heart warmed. 'What are you grinning about, Jude?'

'Just admiring the view.'

'I love boats,' said Tommy, with a mouthful of food. He swallowed hard, then turned to Jude. 'When I'm older, I'm going to get one of my own.'

Harriet nodded. 'It's true. He has a nautical-themed bedroom at home. He's always wanted a boat… and a jet ski, and a surfboard, and a—'

Tommy tossed a pea onto her plate. 'Stop, Mum.'

Jude watched them laugh at each other as Harriet squashed the pea with her index finger.

She's so good with him. They have a nice relationship.

85

Jude's mother was fun when he was a kid. Now all she went on about was money and him working. He knew it was her who got his dad to get him the PA job through a friend's agency.

I would have found my niche without their interference. I guess they thought I'd never work unless they pushed me. PA, yeah right! Like that was ever my dream. I'm with Tommy. I want a boat and to swim and to live by the sea. Hmm, I think I might actually have stumbled across something I can work with right here. Huh! Who knew?

'Jude?'

'Hmm?'

'You seemed a million miles away.'

'Oh, sorry, I was thinking about home.' He saw the glow in her face fade.

'I guess it won't be long before you're back there.'

Do you want me to go back there? Nope, I'm not asking. I'm not ready for that conversation.

He waved out towards the harbour. 'Ah, there's plenty of time left.' He popped a piece of monkfish into his mouth, chewed, stalling for time whilst he thought of a subject change. 'This is a really nice place, Hal. I'm surprised Milly didn't want to bring Keaton here.'

'She wasn't interested in any of my ideas when it came to places to eat. I'm not sure what the restaurants are like where you lot come from, but she has a particular style in her mind.'

'Ah, she's just fussy. I like it here. It's nice. Hey, it's the harbour. What's not to like? Plus, this food is delicious.'

'We're going over to Pepper Bay tomorrow. It's one of my favourite places. They have the quaintest shops and the cutest cottages. I'll take you in Edith's Tearoom. We can ride on the tram to get over there. Milly will love that.' She laughed and rolled her eyes. 'Not exactly a limo, I know.'

Jude laughed and sipped his beer. 'I'm looking forward to doing everything here. I think this little island is great.'

'I bet you've been a few places with Keaton.'

'Yeah, we travel a lot. It's not much fun though. Quite hectic, mostly. And it's so tiring, you know. I can't say I enjoy that side of the job.'

I can't say I enjoy any side of the job. What a nightmare this whole thing has been. Keaton is so messed up. I'm sure he'll drink himself into an early grave.

'I feel as though I've done way too much travelling, Hal. It's not for everyone. The schedules can be tight, and I don't often get to see much of wherever we're at, because work, you know. I often miss sitting at home, staring out at the sea.'

'Do you have a clear view?'

Jude's smile stretched as far as it could go. His heart warmed at the thought of the lone chair on the veranda facing the sunset. 'Oh yeah.'

'I wish we lived on the beach,' said Tommy, shifting in his chair so he was facing his mum.

'We'll have a sea view, one day,' Harriet told him. 'If we dream big and work hard, who knows what we'll achieve.'

'I'll help you, Mum, when I'm older.' Tommy turned to Jude. 'I'm going to get a paper round, and Old Sid said I can work in his fishing shop on Saturdays.'

Harriet laughed as she frowned at her son. 'You can't call him Old Sid. Just call him Sid.'

'That's what Nan calls him.'

Jude watched them chatter about part-time child labour, fitting in swimming times, and their dream home by the sea. They seemed to know what their future looked like.

I can do that. I can get organised and reach for my dreams. What have I been doing all this time? Doing what I was told, that's what.

Being a PA wasn't his choice. He needed to let go of all his parents' expectations and take back his life.

Look at Keaton. He's unhappy. Milly's fighting to be at the top of her game. Harriet and Tommy have a plan. I can totally do this. How hard can it be to change your life anyway?

He needed to think things through. Make a list or something. His job was stable and his life steady. Did he really have the guts to shake it up?

Jude stared over at the boats gently bobbing in the water. Everything about the sea energised him from head to toe. His sister used to joke he was a merman in a previous life, and it wouldn't have surprised him if that were true. He lived for the ocean. Perhaps it was his time to do something about it. Maybe coming to the Isle of Wight was a sign. He glanced at Harriet.

Maybe she is my sign.

Harriet looked up from her plate and smiled before continuing to enjoy her meal.

Jude paid when they had finished, pretending it was part of expenses when Harriet tried to chip in, and then he followed her over to the harbour wall.

Harriet pointed at a beautiful white boat called Lady Silver. 'That's my sister's.' She waved him closer. 'We can sit on the deck, if you like.'

Jude followed her on board and warily looked around for security or someone who might tell them to get off. 'Are you sure we're allowed?'

Harriet laughed and pointed to a newly built complex in the near distance. 'Yeah, she's my sister. Look. She lives over there, and if she goes out on one of her balconies, she'll see us. Then we can wave. It's all right, Jude. I promise.' She gestured at a door. 'We can't go inside, as it's locked. But here's fine. Come on, sit down. It's a bit hard without the cushions, but we won't stop long. Just a moment where we can pretend we have our own boat.'

Tommy giggled as he sat next to his mum and shifted so he was staring at the water gently lapping at the side below.

Okay, now I want a boat even more. What a thought. All three of us together, sailing out to sea. Not a care in the world. Swimming wherever we go. What a beautiful life. To think, some people actually live like that.

He sat by Harriet's side, and curled his fingertips around hers whilst Tommy wasn't looking. She leaned closer and nuzzled her nose into his cheek for a split second, causing him to squeeze her hand.

'So,' she said softly. 'Where shall we pretend we're sailing off to?'

Her tropical scent made him think of turquoise water far, far away. 'White sand, blue sky, colourful fish, untouched coral. We paddleboard, then picnic on deck, and then spend the night gazing at the many stars.'

Harriet rested her head on his shoulder and sighed deeply. 'What should we call our boat?'

'Water Dreams,' whispered Tommy, still staring downwards at the sea.

Jude watched Harriet raise her head. She smiled his way, and he lightly kissed her nose, without making one sound. 'What do you say, Harriet?'

'Works for me.'

He remained locked with her ocean eyes, feeling something a lot more powerful than contentment take over his soul. 'Yeah, it works for me too.'

Tommy broke the moment of companionable silence. 'Can we stay on here till the stars come out, Mum?'

Jude nodded his approval at Harriet, then smiled to himself when she agreed and snuggled further into his chest. He knew they were taking a risk being so close, what with all the reporters running around after Keaton, but right there, in the warm summer evening, he simply didn't care.

12

Harriet

Edith's Tearoom was a quaint, pastel-pink shop in Pepper Lane. Bunting draped in the windows, and pink gingham tablecloths lined the tables, including the two placed outside, as it was another glorious summer's day.

Harriet took everyone inside for a cream tea experience, which entertained her when Milly got in a bit of a pickle with the jam and cream.

'You want me to put both in the cake?' Her nose twitched as her brow lifted.

'Here, let me show you.' Harriet sliced the scone in half, spread some strawberry jam on the base of one half, then added the cream on top and placed the other half of the scone over that, showing them her scone sandwich.

'So, jelly first?' asked Milly, because if she was going to do something, then she had to do it with the utmost perfection.

'Well, that's one rule. It depends on whether you're in Devon or Cornwall. You can put jam on one half and clotted cream on the other and then sandwich them together. If anyone moans about what way up it goes, just flip it.'

Jude breathed out a laugh. 'I don't think mine will last that long.' He took a bite, then leaned over his plate as the jam and cream splurged out the side.

Keaton dipped his finger into his own cream and licked it off. 'Clotted cream is kind of nice on its own.'

'How many calories in this?' asked Milly, suddenly frowning in anguish at her food.

Harriet shrugged. She'd never counted calories in her life, and even if she had, nothing was about to stop her from tucking in to her scone.

Warren sipped his breakfast tea and shook his head. 'Can't I have coffee?'

'Sure.' Harriet stood and waved Jude back down when he went to join her. 'I'll get you one, Warren. Any added extras?'

He shook his head. 'No, just black, thanks.'

She walked over to the glass counter and stared inside at all the tasty goods on offer. Harriet hadn't been in Edith's Tearoom since last summer, and, as usual, everything looked and smelled so good.

'What you after, Hal?'

Harriet glanced up to see the owner, Joey Reynolds, smiling her way. She smiled back at her sister Molly's boss and family friend. 'Hey, Jo. Can I get a black coffee, please?'

Joey's medium-length blonde ponytail swished as she turned to get on with the task. 'Coming up.' She glanced over her shoulder. 'I heard he was here. What's going on, Hal?'

Harriet leaned closer to the counter as Joey placed the hot drink down. 'He's on a break. Thought it would be nice and quiet here.'

Joey noticed someone taking a photograph through the window of Keaton sipping tea. 'Hmm, how's that working out for him?'

Harriet followed Joey's gaze to the front of the shop. 'Well, it's not easy being that famous.'

Joey's taupe eyes twinkled her way. 'You're in the local newspaper, you know.'

Oh heck, I hate lying, especially to my friends.

Harriet felt her stomach clench. 'Yeah, the reporters think he's in a relationship with anyone he talks to.'

Joey flashed a wide smile as she accepted the money for the coffee. 'Heads up, Harriet, my gran has taken your seat.'

Harriet turned to see Josephine Walker holding Keaton's hand, reading his palm. 'Oh, she wouldn't, would she?'

Joey breathed out a laugh through her nose. 'She already is.'

Oh great. What will they think now? I had better go save him from Josephine's fortune-telling skills. Although, Keaton does look interested. Ooh, I wonder if she will see anything in his future about Juliette.

'Hello, Josephine. I see you've met my friends.' Harriet placed the coffee in front of Warren whilst he snapped a shot of his boss having a reading.

Milly leaned further back in her chair, as though trying to escape the old woman. 'Don't think we're paying you, Mrs…'

'Walker,' said Harriet, pulling a chair over from another table.

Milly huffed and folded her arms. 'We didn't ask for palm reading. We're here for cake and sightseeing.'

Jude elbowed her arm. 'Leave her alone. She's harmless. You can be next.'

Milly clenched her hands together as though trying to hide the secrets of her palms from the curious beady eyes glancing her way.

Keaton sniffed and smiled. 'So, Mrs Walker, what you got for me? Am I gonna be rich and famous?'

'It's not this life that makes you smile. It's the old one.' Josephine put his hand to her lap and sighed.

Keaton shook his head. 'Nah, can't say I liked that life much.'

The old lady tapped his hand. 'It just needs a twist, young man.'

Keaton had his polite expression and gentle voice in play. 'You see, the thing is, Mrs Walker, as brilliant as I am, I cannot go back in time to add any twists to my old life. So, I'm afraid, it's gonna have to stay the same.'

Josephine snorted a laugh and gave his hand a slight squeeze with her frail fingers. 'Ah, you know exactly what I mean, exactly what makes you smile on the inside, and just exactly where it is you're supposed to be. You can't fool me, son. I can see her.'

Keaton pulled back his hand, and Harriet could see his discomfort.

'See who?' asked Milly, shifting closer.

Josephine tapped the side of her own nose and panted as she clambered out of her chair. 'I'll leave you to it.' She turned to leave, then glanced over at Jude. 'Be sure you visit Pepper Pot Farm Shop.' She gestured to the shop over the road, opposite the tearoom. 'My grandson owns it. Pop in, won't you.'

Jude smiled politely as he nodded.

'Gran,' called over Joey. 'Leave my customers alone.'

Josephine pointed over at her. 'You're supposed to be resting, Joey.' She looked at Harriet. 'She only had her baby two months ago.'

Harriet clasped her hands together in front of her chest. 'Aww, yes, Mum said. How is she doing, Jo?'

'She's fine, thanks, Hal. Probably sleeping right about now, no doubt along with my husband. Poor Josh is whacked out. Our little Edith wakes up all through the night.'

'Which is why you should be resting, young lady,' said Josephine, sitting back down in the corner.

Joey flapped one hand. She turned her attention back to Harriet. 'How is Kerri getting on?'

'Yeah, she's doing okay. Still at home at the moment, but hoping to move in with Toby soon. Jessica is so good. She only cries for a feed or a nappy change. Mum says we're lucky with her.'

'Tell your mum, I'll pop over one day with Edith.'

Harriet smiled as her small group stood to leave. 'Will do.' She caught Josephine staring at Jude as he left, so she frowned at the old lady, waiting for some intel, but Josephine smiled her way.

Ooh, she knows something. She's got that smug look on her face. I wonder what she saw when she looked at Jude. Oh, why am I buying into any of her nonsense? I wonder if it was about me. Oh, good grief, Hal, get a grip.

She stepped back outside into the warm, sea-salty air and inhaled deeply, smiling at how relaxed she felt. In a trance, she watched Jude edge towards the farm shop until Milly tugged her arm, snapping her out of it.

'Harriet, we need to keep Keaton away from the bar up the end. Look, he's keen. I can tell.'

Harriet glanced up the slope towards The Ugly Duckling pub, then watched as Keaton wobbled across the narrow conduit that ran from the top of the shops down to the small shingle beach at bottom. He jumped over the trickling water beneath him, straightened, and stood in the road, glancing backwards.

Milly quickly went up to him whilst Warren snapped pictures of the shop and beach. 'Ooh, look, Keaton. An art gallery.'

Harriet followed her finger to The Book Gallery opposite the pub. 'Sells books and local art. It's a nice shop.'

Milly seemed pleased. At least, one side of her mouth managed a slight lift. 'Keaton loves art. Come on, let's go check it out.'

Harriet sighed to herself as Milly practically shoved her and Keaton through the opened doorway of the shop.

I wish she'd stop pushing me. And where on earth is Jude?

13

Jude

Jude stepped beneath the blue-and-white striped canopy of Pepper Pot Farm Shop. He waited until the others had disappeared into a shop at the top end of the sloped street, before opening the door and walking inside the dairy shop.

The air felt cooler, and the first thing to catch his eye was a large wooden chicken sitting to one side, homing eggs. He smiled at the beautifully carved statue and started to browse the French dresser awash with conserves.

'Afternoon,' said a female voice.

There wasn't anyone behind the cold counter, home to a large amount of cheese, so he jumped slightly when he heard her. Jude looked over to see a petite lady, with red curls and green eyes, coming out from the back room.

'At least, I think it's afternoon already.' She checked her thin-strap watch and nodded to herself. 'Five and twenty up.'

'I'm sorry, what?'

'It's twenty-five minutes to two.'

Jude pursed his lips and smiled. He lifted his hand and gestured at the shop. 'It's a nice store you have here. I noticed the sign said you make your own cheese.' He moved forward as she waved him closer.

'Come and try some. My husband makes it. We have a dairy farm up the top of Pepper Lane. You should pop in one day. We have visitors come by. Tourists like to watch how it's made, you see. So, we do open days.' She pointed to a sign along the wall. 'All of our opening times are on there. Also…' She handed him a pamphlet from a neat pile on the counter. 'They're on here too. Plus, there is some farm info on there. And our website and Insta page. Here you go.'

Jude took the leaflet and smiled. 'Thanks. Might have to check it out while I'm here.'

'I'm Tessie. Feel free to email or call me to make a booking whenever you're ready.' She placed a small plate on top of the counter. 'Meanwhile, try our cheese. Here you go.'

Jude popped a piece in his mouth and chewed. 'Mmm, it's creamy. So, do you have actual cows?'

Tessie laughed. 'Yeah, we've got cows. Where are you from?'

Jude covered his mouth as he swallowed. 'Oh, erm, California. I'm Jude.' He reached out a hand, and she happily gave it a polite shake.

'You're here with Keaton Byrd. Everyone's talking about him.'

'There's no escape for him.'

'Ah, that's a shame. Where is he now?'

Jude gestured towards the door. 'I saw him go into a shop up the end. It had some books outside.'

'The Book Gallery. Why didn't you go? Don't you like books and art?'

'Erm, I read sometimes, but I'm more of an ocean man myself.'

Tessie beamed a wide smile and tapped over the farm logo on her polo top. 'I love to swim. I go first thing, when the sea is calm.' She pointed to the wall to her side. 'Early morning dip in the sea. You can't beat it.'

'Oh, I agree, but I haven't been out early yet. I might tomorrow, now you've mentioned it.'

'If you want to come out with me, come to the beach at six. There are a handful of us. We've got a bit of a swimming club going on.' She laughed to herself and smiled his way. 'We'll have to give ourselves a fun name soon. Something like the Water Babies or Guppies.'

'What about, the Pepper Bay Barracudas?'

Tessie laughed, and Jude's mind flashed back to his younger years in Malibu. He missed his old swimming club, and his surf club, then there was waterskiing and scuba school. His shoulders drooped slightly and his forehead tightened.

Tessie tapped his hand resting on the counter. 'You wish you were out there now, don't you? I can tell. I know the look.'

Jude admired her observation and laughed quietly. 'Am I that obvious?' He watched her nod and offer more cheese, which he happily took. 'Well, between you and me, I'm thinking about changing careers. I'm a PA at the moment, but it doesn't feel right. It never has.' He glanced out the window. 'I want to work with the water somehow. I'm fully trained in all water sports, and I'm a trained lifeguard. I know first aid, and I can sail.'

'Wow, it seems that's where you should be. You could work round here. Old Pete just left. He used to teach water sports over at Sandly Beach during peak season. Now he's gone, there's an open door.' She stepped back to one heel and showed both her palms. 'Just saying.'

A buzz of excitement almost electrocuted him, it was that strong. What a thought. Being able to do the one thing he loved, in a new place, possibly with a new person in his life. It was worth enquiring about.

'Hey, Tessie, do you know if Pete had a store or some sort of HQ?'

'Yeah, but he sold his surf shop the other month. It's a chippy now.'

'A what?'

'Fish and chip shop.'

'Oh.'

Tessie suddenly clapped her hands and bounced on the spot. 'Ooh, Jude, I've just had a brilliant idea. If you are interested, what about renting the old hut out the back of here?'

He looked behind her as she waved him to the other side of the counter. 'A hut?'

Tessie tugged his elbow. 'Keep an open mind, okay.' She led him out the back of her shop to a narrow walkway and guided him towards the beach.

Jude's mouth opened as Tessie stopped in front of a run-down, blue building about as big as a three-bed caravan.

'Ta-dah!' she announced happily. 'Now, I know it doesn't look like much, but with a bit of a tidy-up and a lick of paint, I reckon you could make this work as your board shop, or whatever it is you would call it.'

'What is this place?'

'It was next door's storage unit back when the shop was a haberdasher's. Old Dolly used to keep rolls of material in here. That sort of thing.' She raised an index finger in the air. 'However, way before that, this place was known as The Old Boat Clubhouse. Look.' She pointed up at a ghost sign above the broken wooden door. 'See, it still says it there.'

Jude mouthed the wording. 'Clubhouse?'

Tessie pulled on the unlocked door, causing it to tilt slightly on its hinges. A waft of dust escaped, making her cough and flap a hand. 'Years back, the fishermen would come here to play cards, drink rum, and talk business. Some say it was a bit of a smugglers' den. Bunch of crooks hiding from the world. Who knows. Well, my dad might, if you're interested. Anyway, it's not much of anything anymore, but it has potential, and history. Come closer. Take a peep inside.'

Cobwebs and dust pretty much summed up the place. Jude could imagine the shenanigans that went on inside all those years ago. He thought about his grandfather, who wasn't anything like his own dad when it came to what side of the law he was on.

I actually like this dust-bucket. Tessie's right, there is potential here. I can hear the sea shanties and almost smell the rum. Oh, I bet they had fun.

Tessie moved around the inside, avoiding some debris on the floor. 'I have a friend, Heath Silver, he's a carpenter, lives up at Silver Wish Farm. If you want to spruce this place up, call him. He's really good. You saw the big chicken in my shop, right? He made that.' She swirled around in the dust. 'He could make a counter, sort out some storage space, maybe. It's worth thinking about. And...' She waved him back outside.

He followed her to the end of a wall to see some shingles, a small slope, and the sea at the bottom.

'Not bad, eh, Jude?' Tessie pointed at the wobbly wall. 'That can go. It's dangerous anyway. Just imagine a bit of space at the end here. You could run your business in the hut, take people down to the sea from here. They can walk around just there.' She showed him the narrow access point. 'We can clear that a bit, put up a sign, and you can get a website up and running. When it comes to water sports like jet-skiing and so on, you can take people around the bay to Sandly. Literally, it's two minutes around the corner. I've swam over to there before.' She nudged his elbow and smiled up at him. 'It's a lot to consider. It's not going anywhere, and I'm sure the owner of the shop next door will give you a good deal on rent. Might even sell it to you, if you ask.'

Jude was blown away by the thought alone. It wasn't what he expected to happen when he woke for a day trip to Pepper Bay. He glanced once more at the old hut as he followed Tessie back inside her shop. 'You know, you're wasted working here. You should be in marketing or something.'

Tessie washed her hands and then snaffled a piece of cheese. 'It's what I do. Marketing and advertising for this place, and I also work for Café Diths. My brother-in-law and his brother are the owners.'

'Oh wow! Those coffee stores are everywhere.'

'So, you see, I could always help you get setup online. Free of charge, as a welcome to Pepper Bay.'

'That's really generous of you. I'll think it over. Meanwhile, would it be possible if we kept this idea between us for now? If I do decide to take this on, I'd have a lot of people I would need to speak quietly to first, so I wouldn't want them finding out before I've even started.'

Tessie tapped the side of her nose. 'Your secret is safe with me.'

'Thanks.' His arm accidentally knocked a model boat on the counter. 'Oops, sorry.' He put it back in place and noticed it had a money slot on top. 'What is this, a savings box?'

'It's a charity box. For the RNLI.'

'What's that?'

'The Royal National Lifeboat Institution. They rely heavily on donations, which is shocking, I know. The whole country is an island, but our sea rescue service is funded by the public and mostly run by volunteers, would you believe? Hey, if you do stick around, you could train to become a volunteer. They'd like you, with all your water knowledge. Check them out online. They have experience days, where you can visit their lifeboat stations, have a chat, find out what it's all about. We have lots of volunteers around here.'

'I would love to do something like that. Thanks for letting me know.' Jude smiled over the counter at her big grin flashing his way. 'Jeez, lady, anyone would think you're trying to get me to stick around.'

Tessie bit her bottom lip, then smiled even wider. 'Word is, you're sweet on Harriet Hadley, and she might feel the same way about you.' She gave him a cheeky wink and a knowing look.

What? How would she know that? Everyone is supposed to think Harriet is Keaton's girl.

'Don't worry,' said Tessie quietly. 'That secret is safe around here too.'

14

Harriet

Watching Keaton eat fish and chips for the first time was amusing Harriet, but she felt she hid it well, tugging back her twitching mouth as much as possible. He kept frowning at the batter and picking it off.

'I've never been a fish man. Don't see the appeal,' he told her quietly, leaning into her arm. He flapped away a hovering wasp, which caused Milly to scream and ask if they could relocate to inside the pub.

Keaton was happy to stay seated in the beer garden of The Ugly Duckling, and Harriet was pleased.

The sun was shining, the outside eating area was quiet, and a seagull was perched on a nearby bench, waiting for Keaton to toss over another chip, which he did without looking.

'This is one of my favourite places to eat,' said Harriet, smiling at Jude, who returned the gesture. 'My sister's partner is the main chef here. He used to be the only one, but he's trained a couple of others now, so that helps him. She lives with him above one of the shops outside. Doll's Gift House. The owner moved in with her partner, so our Molly asked to rent the place. Molly should be around here somewhere. She works here and in the tea shop.'

But I haven't seen her today. I wonder where she is.

Milly cleared her throat as she lifted her glass of pineapple juice. 'Yes, very interesting, Harriet. Now, let's hurry this along and get back to the agenda.'

Harriet's shoulders slumped at Milly's bluntness, but Keaton nudged her arm and leaned in close again.

'I heard back from Juliette,' he whispered.

Harriet completely ignored Milly rattling off the itinerary for the rest of the day and tilted her head towards Keaton to hear more. She moved her face way closer than she had intended and only realised when her mouth came to rest inches from his. Jude clearing his throat, rather dramatically, caused her to jolt back slightly to a more appropriate distance. 'Erm, what did she say?'

He kept his voice as low as hers whilst stopping his smile from taking over his face. 'She gave me her number and told me to call later today.'

Harriet clenched her hands tightly in her lap, squealing with excitement on the inside, as she was pretty sure Keaton wouldn't want her jumping for joy in front of everyone. 'Are you going to call her? You must. Don't leave it. Not now. Ooh, this is huge.'

He shushed her as heads turned their way. He went to carry on with their private conversation but was interrupted by a phone shoved in his face. Keaton flinched as it hit his glasses, and Milly shot out of her chair and snatched the mobile out of the young lady's hand so forcefully, the woman yelped.

Jude stood and leaned over the table, waving Milly down and handing the phone back to its flustered owner. 'Sorry about that. It's just, we have to be on guard around Keaton. Some people can be a bit aggressive with him. We know they don't mean anything, but it's what we have to deal with. I'm sure you understand.'

The lady swallowed hard as she nodded. 'I'm sorry. I was only going to ask for a selfie.'

Keaton lowered his fork with one hand and raised his index finger on his other, nodding at Jude. 'It's okay.' He turned and flashed his winning smile to his admirer. 'Will you tell me if I have food in my teeth?'

She giggled and flapped her hand in front of her face, and Harriet felt embarrassed on her behalf. 'You look good, Keaton Byrd.'

'Thank you. And you are?'

'I'm Dominique. I'm so excited to meet you. I love your films.'

Keaton took her hand and stood by her side. 'Now, how about that picture?'

'Ooh, sure.' Dominique wriggled closer to him and beamed a pearly white smile into her phone. She checked it had come out all right before nodding his way and thanking him for his time.

'It was good to meet you, Dominique.' He sat back down by Harriet and winked when she grinned his way.

Milly pushed her full plate towards the middle of the table. 'How annoying, but what are you supposed to say to them?'

Harriet shrugged as she glanced at Jude, who was busy tucking into a cold chicken sandwich made with crusty doorstep bread. 'They probably won't ever see him again, so they take their opportunity.' She gently nudged Keaton's arm. 'Opportunities should always be taken.' His subtle eye roll didn't go unnoticed, neither did Jude's quick glance in her direction. She saw his controlled sigh and wondered what was going through his mind whilst wishing so badly they were sitting next to each other. She wanted to lean on his arm and snuggle close to his ear to whisper sweet nothings.

We'll have time for that later when Keaton goes off to call his one true love. He'd better ring her. I'll talk to him again once it's quieter. Ooh, I'm so excited. I hope it works out for them. I hope true love really does conquer all.

She blushed slightly and lowered her head when she realised she was gazing dreamily at Jude and he caught her. His eyebrows were a tad raised and his lips twitched to one side. Harriet picked up her glass of water for a sip, purely to cover the soppy grin fighting to reveal itself.

Milly went back to business and that was enough to stop everyone from smiling.

Harriet glanced over at the decking at the back of the beer garden and decided to walk over to feed her crusts to the birds. The warmth of the sun burned into the back of her neck, so she pulled out her sun cream and spread some over her exposed areas before lowering her tortoiseshell sunglasses from her head to cover her watery eyes.

'Hey, how you doing?' Jude's voice was as serene as the setting before her. She remained staring at the tiny birds pecking away on the crumbs on the grass, getting what they could before the greedy seagulls swooped in to take the lot. The front of his shoulder gently touched the back of hers and his chin almost dipped to her neck. 'You want some help with your sunscreen?'

She breathed out a laugh and turned halfway to swipe a blob onto the tip of his nose. Even more of her warmed as his smile beamed her way. 'Jude, I wish it was us here having our lunch together.'

'Are you sure? Because you looked kind of cosy back there with the boss.'

She turned sharply, causing him to take a sudden step back. 'Really, Jude? That's what you're saying to me?'

His gaze lowered submissively and his Adam's apple bobbed. 'I'm sorry, Hal. Please—'

'No.' She snatched her arm away from his approaching touch. 'How can you say that to me? You know more than anyone what it is I'm doing here with you lot.'

He rubbed his hand over the back of his neck as he met her eyes. 'Sometimes, it looks real, okay.'

She leaned closer, gritting her teeth. 'It's supposed to.'

He leaned even closer, clenching his jaw as well. 'Well, I can't say I'm keen on the look.'

'Then don't bloody look.' Her snap caused Milly to whip her head their way. Harriet quickly made her way back to the table and was pleased when Keaton stood, announcing it was time for him to head back to the hotel, even though Milly told him that wasn't on the agenda, and Warren went off on one of his walkabouts, seeing as he wasn't needed.

Jude kept looking her way whilst they waited outside the pub for their cab to arrive, as Keaton didn't want to travel back on the tram.

'Once was enough,' were his words on the subject.

Harriet hoped it wasn't her dad who came to pick them up. She didn't know which cab company Milly asked Elaine to call, but knowing Elaine, she probably would use Ronnie's place.

Oh, I forgot to ask Elaine where Molly was today. I wish I worked at The Ugly Duckling right now. At least my life would be a lot easier.

She glanced at Silver Blooms, her sister Lexi's flower shop.

I'm blaming you for all of this, Lex. You were the one who told me to take a chance on anything that came up. Well, now look. I'm hanging out with a Hollywood film star, who, let's be clear, hates himself and his life, I've got Jude acting jealous, even though he knows it's all fake, and my knickers have been stuck up my bum for the past half hour, driving me insane.

She shifted her legs, trying to release the material, then gave up and tugged at her drawers. She folded her arms in a huff when Milly frowned her way, then pursed her lips when Jude offered a weak smile.

They can all get stuffed. I'm not in the mood for any of this.

She planned on going for a swim as soon as they got back, knowing Keaton was preparing himself for his phone call. She was going to have some me-time before Tommy got out of school.

Oh phooey! I've just eaten. I'll have to wait a while before swimming. Never mind. Ooh, look, it isn't my dad's car. Great. At least something is going my way today. Jude better not try to sit next to me. I'll make sure Milly sits in the middle, as, no doubt, Keaton will sit up front.

Milly got herself a window seat before Harriet had a chance to approach the car, leaving Harriet and Jude side by side, which wasn't so bad. He smelled as good as ever, and his arm was pressed against hers. His fingers lightly tapped his thigh, and every so often his face came close to hers as he turned to gaze out the window.

As soon as the car pulled up around the back of the hotel, Milly jumped out, moaning about the lack of aircon, and Jude grabbed Harriet's hand as she opened her door. He gave her a look that told her he wanted to talk, but she pulled away.

I'll talk to you in a bit, Jude. I need to make sure Keaton makes an important phone call first.

She went to ask him to meet her in his room in ten minutes, but he marched off in the direction of the beach.

Oh, flipping heck, Jude.

15

Jude

After a cool shower, a burger from room service, a text from Milly letting him know Keaton's done for the evening, and no word from Harriet, Jude flopped back on his bed and opened his laptop. He had a whole heap of research to do about the RNLI, then he wanted to check out which licences he would need to set up his business, as he wasn't sure his American ones would count. He would have to prove he had a clean background if he wanted to work with children. Plus, he had to show his first aid skills. He didn't need a bank loan, so that was a plus, but he would have to sort out insurance. It was time to make a list. His PA skills were coming in handy. If there was one thing it had taught him, it was how to be organised. He guessed that was why his mother had pushed him down that route.

I should call her. She'll want to hear about my ideas, especially as I don't plan on going home for a while. Let's see, I'll need a long-term work visa, and I'll have to see what the rules are for buying property here when I'm not a citizen.

He'd never had to think about that stuff before.

Okay, first thing's first.

He sat up, moved his laptop, picked up his phone and dialled a video call to his mother.

'Now I know something is wrong, if you're FaceTiming me.' A smile similar to his own filled the screen, making him pull back.

'Move the phone away from your face. That's it, right back.'

'Wait, honey, let me put it on my desk. Here we go. Is that better?'

The fact he could now see her whole face, including her puffed-up blonde hair, made him laugh on the inside. 'Yeah, that's better.'

'I finished a late breakfast, God, I was starving. Back-to-back meetings all morning and then I had your aunt crying for an hour because Mason left her. Again. I don't know why she keeps taking him back. I've told her a hundred times, but she doesn't listen. What time is it where you are? Have you eaten, honey? What's their food like? I'll have to travel to England one day. I keep mentioning it to your father, but how much he works, I'll be lucky if we get a walk in the park.'

'I want to talk. Have you got time?'

She flapped one hand as the other brought a takeaway coffee cup to her lips. 'I've got twenty minutes till a client arrives. What's up?'

He sighed without her noticing and chewed the inside of his gum for a moment. 'Well…'

'Spit it out, honey. You in trouble? Has Keaton got you into something? I know his lawyers, you'll be fine, whatever mess is happening with him now.'

'No, it's not that. I have an idea I want to run by you. Well, actually, I just want you to know my plans.'

The coffee cup lowered, a perfectly manicured fingernail waggled his way, and Sara Jackson leaned closer to the screen. 'I'm listening.'

'I'm done being a PA. I'm gonna quit soon and start my own business.' He held up a hand, showing his palm. 'Before you say anything, hear me out. I'm not happy in my job. I tried it your way, and it hasn't worked. I want to open my own water sports store, where I offer lessons, sell the equipment, and even build up to having my own brand of sportswear.' He waited a beat.

Sara nodded slightly as she linked her hands on her glass desk. 'You've always been a water baby.'

'And you took me away from that.'

Sara frowned slightly and exhaled a slow and steady breath Jude could hear. 'Now, Jude, what I did for you was what was necessary at the time. You were going nowhere fast. Something had to be done. You needed stability, structure, and to get your head out of the clouds, thinking surfing competitions were all that mattered in life.'

'I could have got sponsored.'

'You listen to me, Jude. I won't take you blaming me for trying to steer you in a direction I thought would benefit you in the long run. You used to be so sloppy and unorganised before your PA training. You only thought about yourself and expected money to fall into your lap. I pushed you into independence and responsibility.'

'It wasn't the life for me though.'

'Hey, being a parent doesn't come with a handbook, you know, son. I've always tried my best to do what's right for you and your sister. Okay, so, sometimes, I might get things wrong, but my intentions are good. Jude, honey, all I want for you is to be happy. I didn't see that in you back then. All I saw was you wasting time in the water when you could have been building a life for yourself.'

Jude ran a hand through his hair, scuffing it to one side. 'I know you meant well, but you didn't listen to me. I'll admit, I wasn't as happy back then as I am now, and, yeah, working for Keaton has taught me plenty. Plus, I'm older now. I've changed. But my love of the ocean hasn't, and I wanna explore that part of me now.'

Sara sat back in her tall leather chair and smiled warmly. 'Okay, Jude. How much research have you done on the business side so far?'

Oh, she's not going to fight me on this. Erm, okay, well, let's see what she says about me staying in England.

'I'm looking into visas, insurance, licensing, and whether I'm allowed to buy property here straight away. I don't need a bank loan, as I have my savings. Plus, I can sell my place in Malibu. That will cover a lot, but—'

'Whoa! Back up, son. You want to start a business in England?'

He shuffled up on the bed and rested his phone on the side. 'I love it here on the Isle of Wight. I wanna stay. Figure it out.' He shrugged and offered a half-smile. 'I can always come home if it doesn't work out, but there's a bit of a gap in the market here. The guy who used to teach water sports on the local beach here retired or left or something. Anyway, I can fill his shoes. It's peak season over here, and school's out soon. This little island gets a lot of tourists, so it's quite a hotspot.'

'Jude, I wasn't expecting you to say any of this, but the staying in England part has thrown me.' She seemed to be mulling it over for a moment and then waved her assistant away when she entered her office.

'If you have to get back to work, we can talk later.'

'No. It's okay, honey. Look, it seems your heart has found a place where it belongs. I can hear the excitement in your voice and clearly see the passion in your eyes. You're right, you're older now, and you've got more life skills under your belt and lots of transferable skills from your PA years. If you think you're ready for a change, then I'm on board. And so is your father when I tell him.'

Jude's brow furrowed as he sat up straight. 'What do you mean you're on board?'

'I'm your mother, Jude. I don't care how old you are, I'll always support you. So, on that note, please don't fret over money. We'll help fund your new adventure. I don't want you to sell your home back here. It will come in handy for your sister when she visits, and you too. I do expect you to come home from time to time.'

He laughed and nodded. 'Of course I'll still come home.'

'Hmm, well. I'm making sure. Now, as for the business side, I'll get Cynthia to delve into all the legal requirements for that country. Just because you hold qualifications here, doesn't mean they're valid there. I'll set you up a file. Don't try to stop me, honey, you know I'm on a roll here. Plus, you know how much Cynthia will love this task. You also mentioned branding. I have a client, who happens to be a good friend, who has her own children's clothing brand. I'll have her people get in touch. She'll know which direction to point you in. I'm thinking, you could start with wetsuits, maybe?'

He shrugged whilst silently laughing to himself at his mother's eagerness to make his business idea a success. He always knew how full-on his family was. If something was getting done, it was getting done the best way, by the best people, and in record time. They were competitive to the extreme, not to mention efficient and dedicated to their careers. 'Thanks, but I can manage all of this on my own.'

'Oh, Jude. You have never in your life been on your own, so that won't start now. If you're into something, we're all into it. I know you think I didn't champion you in the past, but I was at all your sporting events, cheering you on. We paid for your lessons, encouraged you to try your best, wiped your tears when you lost, and helped you stand once again.'

She waggled her finger at the screen. 'You're not to look back at the past and only see bad of us. You had a good life and a good family.'

Jude's shoulders drooped along with his smile. 'I know, but all I'm saying is sometimes it felt as though you weren't hearing me.'

'Oh, I heard you, but I also saw your life. I wanted better for you, that's all. What you're doing now, it looks good. And I believe in you, my baby boy. I always have, and I always will.' She tilted her head and lowered her voice. 'To be honest, I'll be glad when you're no longer around Keaton. That man is going downhill fast, and I don't want you going with him.'

'He's one of the reasons I'm doing this. I look at him and all I see is his unhappiness. I don't want to waste my life trying to fit in where I don't belong. He fell into the life he has now. It was never his goal. I don't wanna be miserable like him. I'm going to attempt to reach for my dream. This feels like my time. I'm ready. Everything about the timing, this place, my ambition fits right now. I can't explain it fully, all I know is I feel calmer since I've been here.'

A moment of silence passed between them as they both reflected on his words.

'Jude. Is there a girl involved in this new story you're building on that island?'

I seriously cannot hide anything from this woman. Should I mention Harriet? I don't want her to think I'm being all wishy-washy over a woman and that's why I'm doing this. Harriet is a big part of my plans, but I would have always gone down this route eventually, just not here, I guess. Hmm, what to say.

'Her name's Harriet.'

'Uh-huh.'

'She has a seven-year-old son.'

'Uh-huh.'

'They both love to be in the water as much as me. We're shaping up to be a great team.'

Well, we were till I got jealous and ruined everything.

'Erm, I haven't told her any of my plans yet. I wanted it to be a surprise. It's still kind of a surprise to me. I want you to know I'm not changing my life because of Harriet. I'm only just finding my feet with her, but I see a life with her and her kid. We have so much potential, and I want to explore that. I want a shot here, with her and with this business idea.' He paused, swallowed hard, and sighed deeply. 'She feels like home.'

Sara's deadpan expression warmed as a soft smile built. Her light-brown eyes almost sparkled as though filled with water. 'You know, when I met your father, it took me all of half a day to pick up on a homely vibe.'

'Yeah, I'm never gonna get over the fact you two met on a beach.'

Sara laughed. 'Maybe that's why you're a beach boy.'

Jude lowered his head and smiled to himself. He always loved hearing about his parents. His dad told more stories about their past than his mother, and those tales never failed to warm his heart. It was magical coming from such love. He and his sister used to say that all the time.

'So, Jude, you know this means your father and I will definitely be coming to England now. We have to meet this new lady in your life.'

'You can wait until I'm more settled with her first. Family meetings come last.'

'Hey, wait a minute. Is she the same girl Keaton has been photographed with over there? Her name's Harriet. I remember now.'

'Yeah, but that's reporters thinking he's got a thing with any woman he says hi to. You know what they're like.'

Now I know how Harriet feels about lying to her family. Jeez, all of this is so damn stupid.

He watched his mother tap away on her laptop.

'Ah, I see. Hmm, she's pretty, Jude. Not sure why there are bikini shots, but when it comes to Keaton, anything goes.' Her attention went back to Jude. 'You be careful, son. You don't want to be a part of any kind of scandal.' She gestured at her laptop. 'They look cosy in some of these pictures.'

I can't tell you. Keaton's privacy rules.

'You can't judge photographs. You know that.'

Please try to read my mind.

Sara took a moment, twisting her mouth to one side whilst humming quietly. 'Okay,' she mumbled, looking straight at him. 'I trust you know what you're doing, baby boy.'

I think she read in between the lines there. Great, well done, Mother. So, that's cleared up, now what?

'Erm, about my new business. You don't have to fund me. I've got it covered, but thanks for the support anyway.'

She flapped a hand as though waving away his comment. 'Oh hush, honey. It's happening. If I can take away any of the stress that will come with this, then so be it. At least now you won't have money worries. So, have you found a store yet, or somewhere to live?'

'I might have a place. I need to speak to the owner. I was gonna ask about renting, but buying would be better. I'll see what's on offer. I haven't thought about where I could live, but it would be nice to have a sea view, I know that much. I'm going to have a look online when I get off the phone to you. See what's available. And, yes, I'm looking forward to all the details Cynthia is about to pass my way. She's a way better assistant than I ever was.'

'Are you sure you want to leave the job with Keaton straight away? Could you do both until you're sorted?'

Jude shrugged. He didn't need to give the question much thought. 'Nah, I'll go all in. He has Milly, and she's really good at her job, so he'll be all right. I'll talk to him soon. Give him fair warning. I just hope I can stay here legally.'

'Hey, both your parents are lawyers. Trust me, son, we'll find a way. Plus, did you know my grandmother was from England? See, you should fit right in.'

Oh wow, so I'm part English somewhere along the lines. I wonder what her life was like here. I wonder what my life will be like living here.

Cynthia's muffled voice entered Sara's office again, and Jude heard a client was waiting.

'You go. We'll speak again soon.'

'Okay, honey. Take care. I love you.'

He returned the kiss she blew. 'I love you too.'

16

Harriet

Harriet's dad's old potting shed seemed to be held together by rust, weeds, and sheer determination. It looked ready to say its final farewell to the well-maintained garden it had resided in for more years than anyone could remember. A good lick of paint, some new hinges, and roof repair were long overdue, but Ronnie didn't seem to mind. His own little haven from the world did him just fine exactly how it stood. Lopsided, with lots of cracks and cobwebs. Not many dared venture into his private quarters, or man cave, as his daughters liked to call it, so Harriet knew he'd be surprised to find her sitting on his wooden footstool, looking a tad worse for wear.

'You all right, love?'

'Hey, Dad.'

His thin lips twitched as his beady blue eyes homed in on her face. 'Are you feeling poorly, Harriet? Your eyes look a bit puffy. What's happened?'

She shrugged and went back to staring at a rather large spider sleeping high up in one corner of the shed. There was no way she was going to be able to take her eyes off the creepy-crawly for more than thirty seconds max. 'I'm okay. I fancied a bit of peace and quiet before dinner.'

Ronnie glanced around his happy place, smiling whilst pulling out a large empty paint bucket to sit on. He stuck a spongey kneepad on top and plopped himself down, facing her. 'Tell me who has upset you, Hal.'

'No one, Dad. I'm just in a quiet mood.'

He breathed out a laugh through his nose, wiped the tip, and raked his fingers through his mop of salt-and-pepper hair. 'My girls don't do quiet moods.' He flapped one hand her way. 'Come on, love. Tell your old dad. What's whirling away inside that noggin of yours?'

Harriet wriggled for a moment on her uncomfortable seat, wondering how her dad managed to sit there for so long each day. A long-drawn-out sigh left her lungs, and she turned her head to see him waiting patiently for an answer as to why she was in his garden shed. 'I don't know, Dad.'

'Hmm.'

'Well, it's just...' She glanced once more at the spider before flopping her head back down. 'I don't know.'

He sniffed and nudged her knee with his own. 'Is it all this malarkey with the actor?'

'Sort of.'

'If you don't like hanging out with that lot, then don't. Let them find another tour guide to show them round the island.'

'Oh, I don't mind that part.'

'So, what's the part bothering you, love?'

She didn't want to talk about Jude with her dad. She didn't want to talk to anyone about him. It was nice having Jude all to herself. Her own little secret. Even though the world thought she was dating Keaton Byrd, which was what they were supposed to think, it was Jude she wanted to be with night and day.

I miss him whenever he's not around me, and I know I'm being daft, but he feels so right. I can't describe it to myself. How am I supposed to tell you, Dad?

'Spit it out, Harriet.'

She swallowed hard whilst shrugging slightly. 'I feel as though things are changing, Dad. My life feels different.' She checked on Charlotte, her name for the spider.

'Life always changes, love. Can't be helped. You got to keep moving along with it, you know.'

Her gaze shifted his way as her heart deflated that little bit more. 'Life in our house never changes. We're always the same, and I like that. Nothing scary happens at home. It's safe here. Stable.'

Ronnie nodded slightly, then gestured at the closed door. 'Life is always changing in our home. Kerri's had a baby. Our Gracie is married. Ashley and Lexi moved out. Even Molly's moved on.'

'Where is she? She wasn't at work today in the tea shop or pub. I thought I'd find her behind the bar, but nope.'

'Oh, she's on holiday, love. Didn't anyone tell you?'

'No.'

'Well, she only left this morning. Your mum will no doubt fill you in over dinner, but, spoiler alert, Molly's in Portugal with Freddy.'

Harriet raised her eyebrows. 'Spoiler alert, Dad?'

He shrugged and grabbed a small brown pot from the side. 'It's what our Lexi says.'

She watched him pull out a bag of soil and scoop some using his bare hands. Her nose crinkled at the thought of having dirt under her fingernails. They were always cut short, as she wasn't one for fancy nails, but she did like them clean and often checked Tommy's to make sure his were too. Some seeds were going in the pot next, and when he seemed satisfied with his task, he set about doing another one.

Gardening gives him the same peace the sea does for me. Ooh, I could do with a swim right about now. I wonder what Jude is doing. I hope Keaton is having a good catch-up with Juliette. Oh, why does life have to be so blimming complicated at times?

'Dad, how did you know Mum was the one for you?'

122

Ronnie stopped planting and stared in thought at his knuckles. 'I don't think I had a choice, love. She picked me. You know what your mother's like.' He chuckled to himself, which caused Harriet to laugh along.

She glanced over at the peeled onion on the windowsill there to help with his hay fever. He swore by its magical powers, so it was nothing new to see one sitting randomly around the house during the spring and summer months. Her mum said he didn't even have hay fever and often removed the medicinal items to add them to dinner.

'You keen on this actor, Harriet? Is that what this is all about?'

Oh my goodness. What a thought. Poor Keaton, he doesn't even love himself, let alone love someone else. Nope, I could never be with someone like him.

Ronnie shook his head a touch. 'Don't answer that. Your scrunched face gave it away. So, if it's not that one, I'm guessing it's the other one. The tall fella. Blondish bloke. Am I right?'

Yep.

'Why does it have to be anyone, Dad?'

He gave her a knowing look, which caused her to sigh on the outside and squirm on the inside. 'What's he done?'

'Nothing.'

'Ah!'

'What does that mean?'

'If only I had a pound for every time one of you girls had boy trouble,' he mumbled, but Harriet heard him loud and clear. 'Look, love,' he added, louder. 'Relationships don't have to be hard. If you like each other, then flow.'

'Did you just say flow?'

Ronnie reached behind a stack of old newspapers and pulled out a small bottle of Irish whisky. He unscrewed the cap and took a sip before offering some to Harriet.

She declined and checked on Charlotte.

'Does he like you back, Hal?'

'It seems that way, but he lives in another country, Dad, and he's going home soon.'

And I'm supposed to be pretending to be Keaton's small-town girlfriend to help with his stupid image. I have contracts and silencing clauses. Money coming my way and a heart already wilting before it's had time to blossom. Great, now I'm thinking in garden terms. That's sitting here in this place. What is that smell? It's not dirt. It's not dust. Probably a dead fox tucked away under all the mess behind me.

She watched her dad take another swig of his drink before putting it away.

'Have you spoken to him about how you feel, love?'

'Is there any point when we won't see each other again for, I don't know, ever?'

'Gets it off your chest, at least. You could always be pen pals. Do people still write to each other?'

I couldn't have any contact with him once he's home. It would break my heart having him so far away from me. Oh, crumble, Hal, don't start crying.

She rolled back the water in her eyes and turned her head away from her dad's view. The dirty window would have to do.

'Look, love, I might not be the sharpest tool in the garden shed, but even I know lots of things can be solved by the simple act of talking. For all you know, he might have plans to whisk you off to America with him.'

Whoa! There's a thought. Would I go? I'm not sure. I definitely wouldn't do that now. We don't know each other well enough for that kind of commitment. Plus, I wouldn't want to uproot Tommy.

Her dad was right about one thing. She should talk to him. Let him know she would miss him so much once he's home. She wanted him to know he was special to her. That he meant a lot.

Fiona's voiced yelled out from the house, informing them dinner was ready.

Ronnie stood, wiping his hands down his thighs. 'Why don't you bring your new friend to dinner one night, love. What's his name?'

'Jude.'

'Well, you tell Jude he's more than welcome.' He laughed to himself as he opened the creaky wooden door of the hut. 'If you think he can handle the Hadleys.'

Mum will marry me off to him the moment he steps foot in the door.

Harriet smiled to herself at the thought warming her soul as she made her way along the garden path towards the house, before having to sprint back to the shed to pick up the onion her mum had called out for.

17

Jude

The knock on Jude's hotel door interrupted his research on the RNLI, which annoyed him, as he was getting to grips with all the volunteer jobs on offer. He hadn't mentioned that part to his mother, as baby steps seemed appropriate. It was one thing to inform her of his business ideas and relocation plans, but he wasn't sure she would be able to take on board the fact her son wanted to risk his own life saving people from drowning, especially if it was because they had gone out in a storm to take photographs of incoming waves.

Another thump hit his door, so he closed his laptop, scrambled off the bed, and went to see who was bothering him at nine o'clock at night.

'Harriet?' He combed his fingers through his dishevelled hair, causing her to gaze in that direction. 'I thought Milly and Warren took you home earlier.'

'They did, but I came back.'

He checked over her shoulder, almost toppling straight into her. 'On your own?'

'Yes. I was perfectly safe, Jude. In fact, I just saw Warren in the bar downstairs with one of the reporters who follow us around. They were drinking cocktails and taking pictures of them. Well, Warren was. I don't think anyone's lurking at this time of the night.'

'You'd be surprised.'

'I think they would all assume Keaton is passed out drunk by now.'

'Have you been up there?'

'No. I've come to see you.' She peered around his body, showing him she was waiting to be invited inside.

Jude was half asleep, half preoccupied with the RNLI, and half amazed to see her. 'Oh, erm, yeah, come in.'

Harriet twisted on one heel and fiddled with the bottom of her pale-grey shirt. 'Are you sure? Only, you don't look too pleased to see me.'

'What?' He frowned in confusion at her still standing in the corridor. 'Of course I'm pleased to see you. Why wouldn't I be? Please, Hal, come inside.'

She walked forward, brushing past his arm with her own, which was one touch too many for him to handle rationally.

Jude closed the door, caught her hand, spun her around, and brought her close into his chest. He dipped his head and lowered his lips onto hers, feeling the warmth inside him move in all directions before settling in his heart.

Harriet let out the softest of moans, which only caused Jude to deepen his kiss. He lifted her, happy she responded by wrapping her legs around him, then lowered her onto his bed.

Oh God, what am I gonna do with this woman? She's killing me here. I wanna strip her naked and make love to her till the sun comes up and then even ignore that deadline.

He brushed back her hair and stared into the ocean in her eyes. 'You're so beautiful, Harriet. So very, very beautiful.'

She stroked along his jaw. 'I came here to tell you I really, really like you, Jude. I want you to know.'

He kissed the tip of her nose, which led to him kissing her cheek and then the length of her neck. Her legs were wrapped around his waist, and he was pretty sure she could tell how ready he was for her. 'I really like you too, Harriet. So much.' He peppered kisses back up to her face. 'So, so much.'

A long passionate kiss overwhelmed them, leaving them heated and breathless. Her hands were clenched in his hair, and his were on her hips, wanting to touch her everywhere.

'Let me do things to you, Harriet. With you.'

'What things?' she whispered close to his ear.

'All things. Whatever you want.'

She wriggled slightly from under him to lean up on her elbows. 'I came here to talk to you.'

He shuffled to an upright position, flashing her a half-grin. 'Not what I had in mind, but we can do that.' He reached out for her hands and pulled her up towards him. One quick kiss later, and he composed himself enough to listen to what she had to say, even though his mind and hands kept wandering to other places.

Harriet laughed softly as she replaced his hands on his lap. 'Jude, stop. We need to talk about stuff.'

He couldn't help himself, he had to kiss her again. A soft peck below her ear. 'What stuff?' he murmured on her warm skin.

Harriet sighed deeply, causing him to sit back and concentrate. It was clear she was worried about something. He crawled to her side and shifted them both so they were side by side, resting against the headboard.

'Talk to me, Hal. What's bugging you?'

Her fingers entwined with his, and her head rested low on his shoulder. 'It's just us, isn't it.'

'What about us?'

'I'm English and you're American.'

Jude breathed out a hushed laugh. 'Yeah?'

'We're so far away from each other, aren't we?'

'You feel pretty close to me.' He wriggled as she nudged his ribs. 'Hey, come on. We're not that different. We both eat hotdogs.'

'You know what I mean.'

'No. I don't, actually.'

Harriet turned to face him. 'We live far away from each other.'

Not for much longer. Should I tell her now? I'm thinking my idea to stick around might actually go down well. Why am I hesitating? It doesn't have to be a surprise. I can share my plans with her. Bounce ideas off each other. Perhaps...

'Jude, it's not going to work, is it?'

'What?'

'Look, I came here tonight because I have stuff I want to get off my chest. I like you so much, and I know we don't have much time left together. I don't want to spend our time fighting. I want to enjoy this summer fling. Make the most of it, you know?'

Jude found himself nodding even though he didn't know at all. Not much was entering his frazzled mind, and his heart had packed up and left the building, leaving behind numbness and a feeling of stupidity.

'Jude?'

'Hmm?'

'Can we do that, please? Can we enjoy each other and then, when you go home, will you do me a favour? Don't contact me.'

Okay, now I'm confused. I thought she really liked me. But now I'm her summer fling? This isn't making sense. Am I missing something here? Does she mean this, or is she just protecting herself?

He pondered over the idea of telling her his plans, thinking it might change things. But then he worried in case it made things worse.

Great! I don't know what angle to take. What does Dad always say? When in doubt, take time to think. Cool. That's what I'll do.

He wasn't going anywhere, so if she was worried about her heart breaking, she would find out soon enough it wouldn't be him holding the hammer.

He leaned over and kissed her hairline. 'I want to spend every moment with you, Harriet. We're gonna have a great time. Make lots of memories, yeah?'

She smiled, but he could see it was weak. 'Yes,' she replied quietly.

And you're gonna get the surprise of your life when everyone goes home and I'm still here. I'll show you, Harriet Hadley. I'm no flake. I've got big plans for you and me. I just hope they make you happy.

'I was wondering, Jude. Would you like to come to my house for dinner one night? My family will be there, just so you know.'

Family meet-and-greet. Now, that doesn't sound like someone who wants to keep things casual.

He smiled to himself and kissed her head as she snuggled back under his arm. 'Yeah, let me know when.'

'I'll speak to my mum. See what suits her.' She glanced up, revealing those beautiful ocean eyes that melted parts of him he didn't know could melt. 'My family can be a bit...' He watched her search for the right word. 'Loud,' she decided on.

'Hey, I work for Keaton Byrd. I can handle anyone and any situation.'

'In that case, you'll fit right in.'

Oh, I plan to. I want to fit with you and your whole family. I'm gonna show you how much you mean to me, and then we'll see exactly how much I mean to you.

He smiled and wriggled on the bed as she leaned over to kiss his temple. Pulling her on top of him, he cupped her face and kissed her with all his building love.

Oh, Harriet Hadley, I swear to God, I'm gonna spend the rest of my life with you.

18

Harriet

The next few days seemed to fly by. Harriet was doing so much with Keaton, but her hands were secretly all over Jude. She couldn't get enough of him. Every touch, every smile, every moment alone they shared was pure magic. They had even managed to wake up together a couple of times.

Her family wasn't buying any of her lies. They knew something more was going on, so she told them about Jude, which helped keep them off her back. The news reports about her life with Keaton didn't help, but her family seemed to understand the stories were just paper talk.

Harriet's mum was the hardest to convince. Jude coming to a family dinner was the only thing that shut her up.

Jude had happily agreed, but Harriet wasn't sure if he was being polite. He had spent every day with her and lots of times with Tommy at the beach, but still she was worried she and her son wouldn't be good enough for him. Jude's life was filled with extravagance, thanks to Keaton, and Sandly sure wasn't anything like Malibu.

'Has our Hal taken you over to see Pepper Bay yet, Jude,' said Fiona, shifting her eyes towards her daughter and adding a mischievous grin. 'It's a real beauty spot. My daughter Molly has not long moved in with her fella over there, and my other daughter Lexi has a flower shop in Pepper Lane, and our Grace lives in Waterside Cottage. Ooh, you have to check out the cottages, they are so adorable.' She scratched her cheek and frowned over at the empty doorway of her kitchen. 'I'm starting to think all my girls will end up over there.'

Harriet smiled to herself. 'I wouldn't mind.' She turned to see Jude smiling her way. 'We've been already. And on the tram. But I was thinking, we could go for a picnic up at Wishing Point.'

'A picnic? Okay, I could get on board with that. I'll speak to Milly.' He looked over the dinner table at Fiona and continued with the polite chatter whilst Harriet fought back her disappointment.

I didn't mean for it to be one of our photoshoots. I don't want to go out for the day with Keaton and the gang. I want to go out and about with you, like a proper couple.

But they weren't a proper couple. She didn't even know what to call their relationship, especially with the whole world thinking she was Keaton Byrd's girlfriend. Part of her heart deflated.

My family think Jude's my new mate and the reporters are making two and two into five. He's worried to show me any affection in public, and Tommy wants him to come to the beach with us all the time. Oh, fail my life.

Baby potatoes were passed under her nose, swiftly waking her from her trance with Jude. Her sister Kerri nudged her arm and leaned in closer.

'Mum will have you married off to him by dessert,' she whispered, adding a cheeky wink.

It was a running joke in the Hadley family that Fiona would marry off her six daughters faster than Mrs Bennet.

Harriet glanced over the mushroom quiche to watch her mother in action whilst her father sat to her side enjoying his dinner as though he were alone. She often admired the way her dad could switch off from the noise that came with the Hadley home.

Jude was being polite. Showing good manners, and Harriet knew her mother was definitely two seconds away from doing a wedding hat search online.

I don't know why she feels the need to tell him about my childhood toys I slept with. How is that relevant to anything? I wonder if he ever slept with toys. Malibu Ken.

She scoffed, almost choking on a piece of sliced cucumber, and quickly raised her glass of water to hide her grin as all heads turned her way.

Jude gave the impression he could read her mind, but she knew he hadn't a clue. Still, he looked cute flashing her warmth in his smile.

'What I don't understand,' said Fiona loudly, which was her normal volume, 'is why the reporters keep saying Harriet is courting that film star.'

Kerri giggled as she turned to rock the pram behind her to send her baby back to sleep. 'Courting, Mum? No one uses that word.'

Fiona shrugged and reached for the salad cream. 'Well, I do, thank you very much.' She nudged her husband, knocking the food about to enter his opened mouth from his fork. 'What do you think, Ron?'

He closed his mouth to lick over his teeth before glancing around the table, looking as though he had woken from a rather deep sleep. 'What?'

Fiona sighed dramatically. 'You know, Harriet, in the papers all month long.' She shook her head, allowing Ronnie to go back to his dinner. 'It's not normal. Can't you tell them, Jude? Put them straight. Let them know you're the one our baby takes home.'

'Erm, I don't take him home, Mum.' Harriet gestured towards Tommy, who was half eating and half playing a game on Kerri's phone.

'Apart from today,' said Jude, smiling her way. 'And I'm glad I've been invited to meet more Hadleys.'

Does he mean that? Is he genuinely interested in me and my life? He'll be off home soon, and that's the last I'll see of him.

She didn't want him to leave. She was already broken hearted just thinking about it. He felt so right and looked at home at the Hadley dinner table.

Mum likes him, and so does Dad, considering he offered to share his jar of mustard. That's a good sign. Oh, but what does any of it matter if Jude goes back to America. I feel so close to him already, and we haven't even slept together. How long can one relationship last with only kisses and cuddles? He doesn't seem to mind, but still.

Jude leaned closer to her and held her hand under the table, bringing her attention straight to him. 'You okay?' he mouthed.

The baby wailed, Harriet jumped, and Kerri stood to make up a bottle of baby milk. Tommy sprinted from his chair, heading for the TV in the living room, and Fiona went over to pick up the baby for a cuddle.

Harriet felt Jude gently squeeze her fingertips. She smiled his way and felt the whoosh of happiness fill her from top to toe when he moved closer and kissed her cheek. 'I'm okay,' she whispered, then caught her dad look away with a smile.

'You have a nice family, Hal.'

She couldn't help herself, before he leaned away, she quickly said, 'Stay.'

He met her gaze with curiosity and gave the slightest of nods, and she wasn't sure if he quite knew the full meaning of her one word.

'Jude,' called over Ronnie, scraping his chair back. 'Come out back with me. I want to show you my veg patch.'

Harriet felt his hand slip from hers as he stood to follow her dad over to the back door. She needed some time alone with Jude to talk about more important things that had started to fill her head and days lately, but right in that moment, Ronnie's runner beans were the main topic of conversation, and she knew Jude would be out there for a while, as anyone who entered her dad's garden would have to listen to the story about the time he came first place in the marrow competition, beating Joseph Sheridan.

Reluctantly, she followed them out into the sunset, scanning the area for any strawberries she could swipe.

As predicted, Ronnie started to talk fruit and veg, competitions and rosettes, and surprisingly Jude looked genuinely interested.

He snuggled up to her side as her dad went over to point up at a plum tree whilst waffling on about topsoils and mulch and other garden stuff she'd learned to switch off from a long time ago. Her waist was tugged closer to Jude, and she turned to see him staring up at the fire-streaked sky.

She rested her head upon his shoulder and smiled when she felt his mouth press onto her hair.

'Stay with me tonight, Hal,' he whispered close to her ear.

She glanced his way and could immediately tell he wanted more than a night filled with kisses.

19

Jude

Twinkling stars filled the inky sky as Jude and Harriet walked back to the hotel, taking as many back roads as they could to avoid prying eyes. They were both getting fed up with all the attention and chaos that came with Keaton's life, and the fact they had to steal moments for themselves, hiding away in the shadows like criminals.

Jude wished they were walking along the beach. He would hold her hand, kiss her under the moonlight, tell her how deeply he was falling for her as their bare feet sank into the cold sand, without a care in the world.

Instead, they were dodging reporters, scuttling along walls like rats, jumping at their own shadows, and acting like banned lovers. It was getting ridiculous, and Jude was ready for it to stop.

I want normal. It's time.

He stopped her from their speed-walk, pulling her closer to his chest. 'I can't make it stop, Hal. If I could, I would. I want you to know that. But you signed a contract, and we have to see it through, no matter how much I hate this crap.'

Harriet stroked over his chin for all but a moment. 'Hey, it's okay. I understand. I don't like hiding as though I'm having some sort of sordid affair. It's not giving us much of a chance to have fun.'

'That's why I prefer it when we're out on the water. It seems so far away from life, and no one cares if we're swimming or paddleboarding. There's nothing else for them to see but that.'

'It'll be over soon. Milly said it was only a few weeks. I know it's dragging, but there isn't much left, and then...' She paused and looked at her feet.

'Then what, Hal?'

'You'll all go home.'

He shook his head as he raised her chin with one hand. 'I don't have to. I have vacation time due. I could stay longer. All summer, in fact.' He waited to see what kind of reaction that would provoke. Judging by the smile in her eyes and the tight grip she had on his top, he guessed she was pleased.

'That would be lovely, Jude.'

'I'll make it happen.'

'You sure you can?'

He knew he was taking a risk, lying to her about his plans, but he lowered his head and kissed her tenderly on the lips anyway. 'I'll make it happen.'

They carried on with their journey back to the hotel, sneaking in the staff entrance around the back, as there was a lone photographer sitting on a bench out the front, eating a sandwich and drinking coffee.

The lift door closed them in and just as Jude went in for a kiss, his phone pinged him back into reality. He groaned at the message, sinking his shoulders lower into his body in a slump.

'What's wrong?' she asked softly.

He pointed up above and then pressed another button on the panel. 'I've been summoned.'

Harriet entwined their fingers and pulled him close for a cuddle, banishing his disappointment immediately. 'Do you want me to come with you?'

'No, it's okay. You can get ready for bed, and the thought of you in my bed will keep me awake while Keaton chews my ear off about whatever he needs next.'

'What do you think he wants this late?'

'Who can tell with him. Probably more vodka.'

'Hey, don't be so harsh. He can't help the way he is, Jude.'

'Really? You're making excuses for him now.'

Harriet sighed and stepped outside the lift when it came to Jude's floor. She reached out for the keycard and smiled weakly. 'There's more to him than people see.'

Jude's foot was holding the lift door open. 'Yeah, I know more than anyone, but it doesn't take away the fact he mostly acts like a spoiled brat, and one that constantly needs saving.'

She gave him a slight wave and took a step back. 'Go on. The sooner you see him, the sooner we can go to bed.'

He watched her enter his room before allowing the lift door to close, taking him the rest of the way to Keaton's floor.

'Jude, where you been, man?'

Having a great night with my girlfriend. Wait… is she my girlfriend? It does sound nice, but I'm not sure we're going steady. Does this need a conversation? And why is Keaton wearing a leather jacket with just his underwear?

Jude pointed over at his boss, who was busy taking a swig of vodka straight from the bottle. 'Where did the jacket come from?'

And why is that my leading question? Man, I've been working with this guy for way too long if I'm not even making the half-nakedness the focal point.

Keaton slapped one hand to his collarbone. 'This is how I used to dress before I was famous and had to do what I was told,' he slurred.

'You? Doing what you're told? Okay. How about we get you into something more appropriate for bed and you get some sleep.' He tried to wrestle the bottle of alcohol from Keaton, but even when drunk, Keaton had a mighty grip.

'You know I love you, right, Jude?'

'Hmm.'

'Well, you need to stop touching my drink, otherwise I'll stop loving you. And then what?'

Then I'll probably get some peace and quiet in my life.

He scrunched his eyelids and flopped onto the sofa, not caring how deflated he looked.

This is going to be a long night, and no doubt Harriet will be fast asleep by the time I get to bed. Great!

He pressed his head backwards as Keaton started to mumble something about someone called Juliette, a hospital, and Harriet. None of which made any sense. There were some words about love, and others about small-town life, and it wasn't easy for Jude to piece them all together. The fact Harriet's name kept coming up confused him even further.

Why the hell does he keep mentioning her in the same sentences as love and... Whoa! Did he say marriage? Oh, please, no. Do not tell me he has fallen for Hal, and he's thinking about proposing.

He ran his fingers through his hair and closed his eyes, trying to drown out Keaton's slurred nonsense.

There is no way Harriet would go for that charade or for real. But no one says no to him. She would. I have to believe she would. But why was she sticking up for him tonight? Have things changed? Have I been so wrapped up in my own feelings for her I missed vital signs. Oh, I need some sleep. Why is he singing? Please, make it stop.

'Keaton. Keaton.' Jude peeled himself off the comfy sofa and started to guide his boss to the bedroom. 'Come on. It's time for bed. Everything will feel better in the morning.'

Keaton groaned and hiccupped out a laugh as he let Jude support his weight. 'I love her, you know.'

Great.

'Sure. Let's get you into bed.'

Keaton pulled his black jacket around his chest. 'I'm refusing to take this off, so don't even try.'

Jude lowered him to the bed and stepped back to look at the slumped mess before him.

Aw, Keaton, you're so much better than this. I wish you would get help.

He tugged the vodka bottle away as Keaton closed his eyes.

'I love her,' Keaton mumbled.

Jude turned to the doorway to see Milly standing there, holding her side as though she had a stitch.

'I was at my cousin's house when Warren called,' she whispered. 'Why has he got into this state?'

Jude shook his head as he passed her by. 'I don't know. Something's got him rattled.'

Milly sighed quietly as she entered the bathroom. 'I'll get a bucket, in case he hurls during the night.' She wiggled her fingers his way. 'You can go back to bed, Jude. It's my turn to stay up with him.'

How the hell Milly kept track of turns was beyond Jude.

She must keep notes.

He wasn't about to argue when Harriet was waiting in his bed. He needed to make the most of the time they had together; it could be short lived if it turned out she was tempted by the luxury Keaton could provide.

Please, Hal, don't fall for the sugar-coated bullshit.

He headed for the lift, inhaling big gulps of sweet carpet spray or whatever it was filling the hotel. His heart was racing and his head was aching at the thought of Keaton asking Harriet to marry him.

'Well, you're not gonna let it happen,' he told the inside of the lift. 'This isn't part of the plan. No, sir. He can find his own woman, because he sure as hell isn't getting mine.' He clutched the side of his head, gripping his fingernails into his hair as the lift brought him to his floor.

Breathe, Jude. Just breathe, man.

He stared hard at the door, not wanting to open it. Not wanting to go inside, but it opened anyway, with Harriet on the other side, staring up at him in shock.

'Flipping heck, Jude. You scared me. I was about to come up to see if you needed any help.'

He entered and waited for her to close the door. 'Look, Hal, he was drunk, mumbling about love and marriage. I think he might propose to you. I don't know. He wasn't exactly coherent. But your name kept coming up at the same time as him mentioning loving someone. I assumed, maybe you.' He slumped to the bed and held his head.

Her hands glided around his, pulling them close to her body. 'Did he say any other names?'

He lifted his head up, knowing full well she would see his deflated expression. 'Erm, Juliette, I think.' He had no idea why Harriet was smiling. There wasn't anything much to smile about. As if things couldn't be any more absurd, Keaton was going to suggest a fake marriage, or maybe a real one. Who could tell with that man.

Harriet lowered herself to her knees, settling between his legs and nudging his nose with her own. 'She's his high school sweetheart. I got them back in touch. He's always loved her, but you can't tell anyone.' She placed a hand over her mouth as her eyes widened. 'Am I allowed to say that? I'm in trouble now, aren't I? I don't think I'm allowed to say anything about his life, and I went and told you about his secret crush.'

'It's okay. It's just me. As a team member, we tell each other everything so we're all up to speed, and as we're all under the same agreement, it doesn't go any further than our circle. And… Wait, what? He's speaking to some woman from his past and keeping it a secret?'

Harriet shrugged and settled back on her heels. 'I think so. He was waiting for her to message him back. We wrote to her on Facebook.'

Jude's eyebrows went as high as they could. 'Anyone could hack into that, Hal.'

'He didn't seem to mind. Plus, she wrote back. I think things might be going well.'

Jude pointed at the ceiling. 'Might explain the jacket, but not too sure about the state he was in.'

'I don't think he can give up the booze, Jude. He's going to need professional help.'

He stood, offering his hand to help her up. 'I need to call Milly. She has to know about this in case we have to do damage control. Jeez, Hal, you can't help him with crap like that. His life has controlled areas. He's not your average Joe, which means he can't go around doing average stuff like the rest of us.' He reached for his phone as Harriet approached the window to stare outside at the dark sky.

'It's so sad, Jude. From what he told me, she's a good person, and he still loves her. And I told him to go there. Donate to a local hospital or something. She's a nurse, you see.' She spun around and grabbed the phone before he dialled Milly's number. 'Please, help him, Jude. Give him a chance at real love. Juliette might be what he needs.'

He sighed heavily and lowered his phone. 'Okay, Hal. I'll help him do this the right way.' Her smile warmed him, but he knew Keaton making a success of his life outside of fame and money was a longshot.

Jude didn't want to get involved anymore. He wanted to spend his time making plans, getting his business up and running, and train for the RNLI. He hadn't even found out if he could stay in the country yet, and now he had Keaton's long-lost love to figure out.

I need to quit, and I need to get on with it fast. I'm gonna speak to him tomorrow. And I'll tell Milly about this in the morning. Meanwhile, this woman hugging my chest is all I need to focus on. She's not marrying Keaton Byrd. I'm not about to lose her to Hollywood life. But, what I am about to do is kiss her till we both pass out.

Harriet laughed on his lips as they came crashing down upon hers. 'I guess this means we're ready for bed now?'

'Always ready for bed with you.'

20

Harriet

Harriet was whispering with Milly in one corner of Keaton's room whilst Jude supervised him in the shower. Harriet was surprised Jude's job stretched that far. She and Milly had found a private rehab centre close by to where Keaton grew up, and Milly had booked him in. It was happening sooner than expected. They were leaving the Isle of Wight. Between them, they would talk Keaton into going home to get clean, and Harriet was quite sure using Juliette would be what convinced him to take up the offer.

Harriet could hear the water running in the next room and Keaton's muffled voice. She tried not to think what was going through the poor man's mind. Rehab seemed scary. She wondered if Milly contacting Juliette on the quiet was the right thing to do after all. It was done now, so they couldn't back out, but she was sure Keaton would have something to say about her interference at this level.

Milly nudged her arm, giving her a reassuring almost-smile. 'Hey, Juliette seems like a good person. She's going to be there for him every step of the way. Once Jude lets him know that piece of vital information, Keaton might thank you for telling us about her.'

'I doubt that, but thanks for trying to settle my stomach.' Harriet's knees weakened as the shower switched off. She swallowed the hard lump in her throat and made her way over to a chair to sit down.

Keaton's yell practically shook the room, causing Milly to jump and Harriet to swallow hard again. 'She did what?'

Jude's voice was less easy to hear, so neither of the women knew what was going on until Keaton stepped out of the bathroom to face them.

Oh my goodness, he looks so mad. I don't think he's going to pay me now. Probably sue me for everything I've got, which isn't a lot. I wonder if my old stamp collection is worth much.

'Harriet, what the hell?' Keaton stomped forward, wearing only a white hotel towel around his waist. He almost punched one fist to the side of his head. Then he scanned the room as though looking for something.

'There's no vodka,' announced Jude, stepping in between his boss and Harriet.

'I'll make coffee,' said Milly quickly, disappearing to do so.

Keaton manoeuvred to the sofa, keeping his glare fixed on Harriet. 'You wanna explain what the hell happened between me falling asleep and waking up?'

'Juliette cares about you, Keaton.' Harriet sniffed, straightened her back, then stood. 'Hey, you need someone who actually cares about you. What? You don't think she knows what you've become? You think she's the only person on the planet who hasn't seen the state of you?'

Keaton's bloodshot eyes widened. 'Oh, jeez, Miss Hadley, don't hold back.' He waved his fingers her way. 'Finish, why don't you. Tell me more about my pathetic life.'

Harriet flashed a look at Jude, sighed to herself, and then settled at the other end of the sofa. 'I'm sorry, Keaton. I shouldn't have said it that way, but I think you're in a great position to turn your life around. I mean, really change everything. And the best part is, Juliette wants to help.' She took a moment to see how he would respond, but he folded his arms in a huff and stared at his towel. 'This is a good opportunity, Keaton. Please, take it. Go to rehab, see Juliette again, give yourself a chance.'

Jude leaned against the window and stared at his boss. 'Harriet's right. You should do this. This will be good for you. Milly's on board too.' He shook his head slightly, giving the impression he was talking to himself. 'Look, Keaton, you need help, man. Take the shot. Don't waste any more of your life. We all know how much you hate the way things are for you, so why not take a leap. I know it's a hard road, but I believe in you. You'll get through this.'

'You don't need a Hollywood life,' added Harriet softly. 'You need a happy life, and the one you have now isn't working.'

Keaton shifted on the sofa and unfolded his arms. 'I don't need you two, or Milly, going all therapist on me. I already know my life is shit and has to change.' He twiddled with the top of his towel. 'It's easier said than done, that's all.'

Harriet reached over and gently rested her hand over his. 'We can only imagine, which is why you need to be surrounded by experts.' She gave his fingers a soft squeeze. 'And by someone who cares about you. The real you.'

Milly came back with coffee, which Keaton begrudgingly took. She took a step back, opened her tablet, then raised her eyes to meet his. 'I've got you in. Our flight is due in a couple of hours. You can cancel, of course, it's up to you, but just know Juliette is waiting at the other end.'

Keaton sipped his coffee whilst Harriet glanced over at Jude.

Harriet knew if Keaton agreed, Jude would probably go with him. He'd want to settle Keaton at the rehab centre. She couldn't be entirely sure. All she knew was she wasn't prepared.

This is my own fault. I was the one who got Keaton into this situation, making myself busy. He was just so sad, not to mention lonely. Oh well, at least one of us might stand a chance at a happy ending. Say yes, Keaton Byrd. Be braver than me. Go change your whole life and make yourself proud.

Jude pushed himself away from the window. 'What do you want, Keaton? Tell us our next move.'

Milly made some sort of high-pitched squeal, sounding as though she were being choked. All heads turned her way, and she raised her phone. 'Well done, Jude,' she snapped. 'A picture is going in tomorrow's paper of you kissing Harriet.'

Keaton blew out a husky laugh as Harriet lost all words.

Jude turned to his boss. 'Erm—'

'Save it,' said Keaton, clearly not in the mood for another subject crowding his thumping head. He nodded at Milly. 'Let them know she's his girl. Tell them she just held my hand when I felt wobbly on my feet. Hit them with rehab and retirement. That'll keep them off her back.'

Jude stepped closer to Harriet but remained staring at his boss. 'Wait, does that mean you're going to go to rehab?'

Keaton took another sip of his coffee, clearly mulling over his options. He stood and made his way back to his bedroom, swiftly followed by Jude. 'Yeah, I'll go.' His voice was barely audible, but they all heard, and Jude gave Harriet a tight smile before disappearing into the other room.

Harriet turned to talk to Milly, thinking an explanation was due, but Milly was already on her phone, making calls and organising Keaton's life choices.

Just me again, I guess.

Harriet wasn't sure how she'd feel when they all left. Things would certainly be quieter. She'd actually miss Keaton, and Milly. Jude, she couldn't even think about.

Finally, people will stop thinking I'm seeing Keaton. At least I can get back to normal now.

Jude poked his head around the doorframe, looking at Milly. 'Call Tarik, have him meet you at Keaton's plane at the stop-off. I want him there. I want you both there.'

'Who is Tarik?' asked Harriet, purposely avoiding eye contact with Jude in case she cried.

'His main bodyguard,' said Milly, still glued to her phone. 'And his friend. A real friend. He doesn't have many, but they exist.'

Harriet nodded and controlled the sigh desperate to leave her tight lungs. She sat in silence for a while whilst Jude and Milly buzzed around her, making arrangements, talking procedures, and checking on Keaton every ten seconds.

Milly finally put her phone away and gestured to the bedroom. 'I'll pack his things, Jude. You go do yours while I'm here, then when you get back, I'll go do mine. We'll have some breakfast brought up before we head off.'

Jude stopped her. 'I'm staying here, Milly.'

Wait, what?

'What do you mean, Jude. We have to get Keaton to rehab. You can't stay here. Everything is sorted.'

Jude glanced at the bedroom door, then at Harriet, before turning his attention back to Milly. 'I've quit my job, Milly. Keaton knows. It's okay. He has you, and you know what you're doing. Tarik will join you, and you'll have Juliette's support at the other end. Everything will work out. Keaton isn't the only one wanting life changes. I do too. I've got my own plans. My own dreams, and I'm not wasting any more of my time.'

Milly looked just as shocked as Harriet. More surprisingly she appeared cheesed off. Harriet was sure

Milly would jump at the chance of taking Jude's job. Perhaps go as far as to do a cartwheel.

Milly stormed off to the bedroom, leaving Jude to turn his attention to Harriet. He plopped himself on the sofa and reached out for her hand.

'Jude, I know you said you would use your holiday time to spend the summer here with me, but if Keaton needs you to go with him, please don't feel you have to stay because of me. I know how vulnerable he is. I don't want to be part of anything that doesn't help him.'

'Harriet, listen to me for a moment. This wasn't how I planned this conversation. To be honest, none of this was planned. Coming here was a spur-of-the-moment decision. Meeting someone like you wasn't what I was expecting. The Old Boat Clubhouse certainly wasn't on my to-do list, but just like that, it all came together like it was meant to be. I'm not prepared to walk away.'

'Jude, I have no idea what you're talking about.'

He moved forward, and Harriet felt the butterflies in her stomach shift. 'I'm staying here, Hal. Now, I need you to tell me you'd be happy about that.'

'Do you mean for the summer?'

Jude shook his head and smiled warmly. 'No, Hal. I want to settle here. Start a business. Hang out with you every day. Buy a home overlooking the sea. Relocate. Change my life.'

Harriet placed her free hand over her chest. 'For me?'

Jude gave a half-shrug and grinned. 'Partly. Some of it is my dream anyway. I figured, after meeting you, I could carry out that dream right here, or rather, over there in Pepper Bay.' She followed his hand pointing at the window.

'Pepper Bay?'

He nodded and kissed her knuckles. 'As soon as they leave, I want to show you something.'

Harriet was slightly dazed by the morning's events. She was starting to wonder if she hadn't woken up at all. 'Erm, what do you want to show me?'

'The Old Boat Clubhouse. The owner has agreed to sell the place to me.'

21

Jude

Jude and Harriet were enjoying ham sandwiches in his room whilst chatting away about The Old Boat Clubhouse. They were eager to get over there to take some measurements and make layout plans. Harriet was full of ideas, which only made Jude even more sure he had made the right choice.

Harriet smiled through her white crusty bread, then lowered the sandwich from her lips. 'You know, if push comes to shove, I can always marry you so you can stay in the country.'

'Oh, is that right?' They both laughed, and Jude took her hand. 'Thank you, but I don't want to be a green card, or whatever you call it over here. Anyway, I think it'll be okay. There are lots of Americans living and working here. I can't see there being a problem.'

Harriet flapped her sandwich and flopped it back onto the plate. 'Let's go to Pepper Bay now. I'm far too excited to eat.'

Jude breathed out a laugh as he stood to wipe away some crumbs from his shorts. 'So, how much do you know about this place already? I like to find out history on places.'

'Well, it's behind Dolly's Haberdashery. That's what the shop used to be called when I was growing up. It got divided into two shops. Doll's Gift House, and Pepper Pot Farm Shop. I've not actually seen the building myself, because it's right around the back of the shop and no one really goes there. I've heard some old stories though. Mostly from

Grandad. We should speak to him, or Nora. She's his friend, and she knows everything.'

Jude went to speak, but Harriet's phone started to vibrate, gaining her attention. 'You take that, Hal. I'm going to the bathroom before we leave.' He watched her nod his way before he closed himself inside the en suite.

Whoa! I can't believe how much my life is changing. Kind of feels a bit surreal. I don't feel backflip-happy, but definitely peaceful-happy. This is new. I guess that's why I can't explain this properly to myself.

He flushed the toilet, washed his hands, and smiled at his reflection in the mirror. A thud on the bathroom door made him jump. He quickly swung it open as Harriet yelled his name. Her eyes were watery and filled with fright, and her face was drained of all colour.

'Jude, that was the school. It's Tommy. He's run away.'

'What?'

Harriet grabbed her bag from the chair whilst trying to tug on her left trainer. 'I need to get home in case he's gone there. The school have called the police.'

Jude grabbed her waist as she tumbled into the wall. 'I'll come with you.' He slipped into his pumps and followed her out the door. 'Have you called Fiona yet?'

Harriet waited till the lift brought them to the lobby. 'I need to call everyone.' She slapped the phone to her ear as she ran out into the dreary street.

Jude quickly guided her around the side to where Keaton's hire car was parked. He still had full use till the end of the month, and Harriet needed to get home fast.

Harriet's voice was trembling down the phone as she spoke to family members, and Jude had never felt so useless in his life. He concentrated on the short drive to her house.

Not wanting to break the speed limit, especially as it was drizzly outside.

A moment of silence filled the car, only interrupted by the occasional swipe of the windscreen wipers. Jude reached one hand over to rest it upon Harriet's leg, and she glanced his way, revealing a whole heap of worry and exhaustion.

'Hey, we'll find him, Hal. He can't have gone far.'

Harriet shook her head slightly as though talking to herself. 'I don't understand, Jude. Why would he run out of school? This isn't like Tommy at all. Nothing makes sense right now.'

Jude pulled up behind a police car outside her home to see Kerri in the doorway, waving them towards her. Harriet was out of the car before he'd had a chance to remove his seatbelt.

Jeez, this doesn't look good. I hope the police find him soon. Harriet's about two seconds out from having a breakdown.

'What's going on?' he asked Kerri as he approached.

Kerri had the same look on her face as Harriet. A tear escaped her worried blue eyes as she waved him closer to the hallway. 'We don't know much yet,' she whispered.

Jude handed her a tissue from his pocket and followed her into the living room. Two police officers glanced his way before returning their attention back to Fiona, who was handing them a school photo of Tommy whilst describing his uniform and face.

Harriet sat to the female officer's side and grabbed her arm. 'Please tell me what you're doing to find my son.'

'We've put word out all over the island. He won't be able to board the ferry without being spotted. Now, Miss Hadley, I need you to tell me where his friends live, in case he has gone to one of their houses.'

Fiona cut in before Harriet had time to answer. 'His friends are all in school. Where he should be. So, they won't be home, and Tommy will know that.'

The female officer smiled politely at Fiona, then turned back to Harriet. 'Has there been any problems at home recently? I know people don't like being asked, but we have to know. We need to try and figure out why he would have left school out of the blue. Your mum was telling us before you arrived that this is out of character for him.'

Harriet nodded. 'It's true. Tommy has never done anything like this before. I don't know what he's thinking.' She went to continue but her sister Ashley pushed past Jude in the doorway to sprint inside.

'Dad's got the whole cab company driving round looking for him, and I've just come from the park.' She shook her head at Harriet. 'Lexi's checking the harbour, and Tessie has informed all of her WhatsApp groups.' She stared at the male officer. 'She has a Pepper Bay one and a Sandly one. Word is getting out. Soon, everyone on the island will be searching for our Tommy.'

Fiona pursed her lips as she nodded her approval towards Ashley. 'I've got Queenie on the lookout down by the ferry port, and Bryce called to say he's hired a helicopter to fly over.' She turned to the police. 'He's rich.'

Jude swallowed hard as Harriet's frightened gaze came his way. He manoeuvred through the small gathering to find his way to her side. He lowered to the carpet and rested his hands on her lap. Her head rested on his for a moment before she sprung back to life as though getting a second wind.

'I need to be out there.' She gently moved Jude and stood, turning to the female officer as though looking for some sort of confirmation.

Jude stood and placed his arm around her back.

155

Christ, she's shaking. I don't know what to do. How can I help? Think, man, think.

He tugged her closer to him and kissed her head. 'He's gonna turn up, Hal. He will.'

Harriet ran to the door. 'Have you checked Dad's shed?'

Jude ran after her to find her deflated in the garden when she discovered nothing in her father's shed but the standard junk, soil, and onions.

Harriet clutched at her stomach. 'Oh God, I feel sick.' She slumped sideways, placing one hand towards the shed to balance herself. Tearful eyes flashed his way. 'What if his dad's come back and taken him, Jude?'

'No, don't think that way. He wouldn't be able to do that. He would get into trouble with the law. Surely he would know that.'

Harriet shook her head and straightened her posture. 'I don't know what to think. My brain feels like it's been fried.'

Jude stepped forward and cradled her into his arms. 'Has he given you any reason to think he would come here and take Tommy?' He felt her head turn on his chest.

'No. He has no contact.' Her face moved up his top. 'I don't know what to think. The school has security cameras, and they didn't show anyone lurking around. Just Tommy climbing over the gate.' She stepped back and lifted her arms. 'What kind of a gate is that? Kids shouldn't be able to climb over.' A wagging finger flapped close to his face. 'I'm going to report it to the school board or whoever.'

Jude took her shaky hand and pulled it to his chest. 'Hey, how about we drive round ourselves? Fiona will stay here in case he turns up.'

She nodded and took a breath. 'I can't think where he might go. Grace is on lookout at the Donkey Sanctuary. He loves the donkeys, but I… What about the beach?'

They both looked up at the dreary sky.

Fiona called out from the back door. 'Harriet, I've checked his things. He's been back here. I know, because his wetsuit is missing.'

Jude followed Harriet back inside. Ashley was explaining to the officers that Tommy's wetsuit was his most prized possession and he wouldn't go anywhere without it.

'So what does that mean?' asked Kerri, gripping the top of her white-blonde pixie cut. 'He's got it into his head he's not coming back home?'

A breath flew out of Harriet as she tried to scurry past Jude to get out of the house. He turned to Fiona. 'We'll check the beach. He might have needed some head space.' He wanted to explain more about how the ocean had an effect on people like Tommy. He knew because he was the same. Harriet as well. But he ran outside to the car, where Harriet stood, taking deep breaths.

They got in and pulled away. Harriet was glued to the window, and Jude was hoping the rain would disappear and Tommy wasn't in the water whilst the waves were rough.

He wouldn't, would he? No. He's been educated on the sea. He knows the rules. Jeez, my guts are churning. Please, please, don't let him be in the water.

The beachfront was pretty much empty, thanks to the weather. Some small crowds filled the amusement arcades, shops, and restaurants, but the beach huts were closed up, and there was only one man and his dog walking the promenade.

Harriet rattled each hut, just to be sure, then screamed out Tommy's name towards the damp sand before them. She ran to the shoreline, peering out to sea, and Jude joined her side, wishing they had binoculars.

'I can't see anyone out there, Hal.'

She shook her head. 'No, nor me. Keep looking.'

Jude jumped as she screamed out Tommy's name once more. The wind was picking up along the front, causing the waves to grow and the spits of rain to slap into their faces. The sky was darkening, threatening more to come, and Jude wished even more he was already a member of the RNLI.

'Should we call the coastguard, Hal?'

'There's no evidence he's out there. Mum's probably called Bert, anyway, now she knows Tommy's taken his wetsuit. Bert will get a crew out.' She scanned the water again. 'Oh God, Tommy, where are you?' She started to hyperventilate.

Jude grabbed her as she fell to her knees. 'Breathe, Harriet. Just breathe. Focus on me.' He lifted her chin to meet her weary eyes. 'Breathe. In. Out. Slowly. You've got this. Just breathe.' He sat with her for a while, breathing slowly along with her, helping to bring back the control. Once she was able to draw breath properly, he held her close and stroked her wet strands of hair. Her limp body was shaking as hushed sobs vibrated on his shoulder.

Harriet suddenly pulled away and stood. 'I can't fall apart, Jude. My son is out there somewhere, and he needs me to be strong.'

Jude joined her side as they made their way back up to the beach huts. 'You're doing great, Hal. And this will all be over real soon. I promise. You'll receive a call any minute to say he's been found safe and well.'

Harriet almost smiled, but then her phone rang, surprising them both. She quickly answered the call.

Jude listened as he watched her facial expressions change from hopeful to confused to annoyed. He waited patiently for her to finish on the phone. 'What's wrong?'

'That was Tommy's teacher. She's found out what made him run away. Apparently, the kids in the playground got wind of Keaton leaving to go back to America, and one lad has only gone and told our Tommy I've gone too.'

'What? That's crazy. As if you would leave him behind.'

'I know. But he doesn't. He should, but he's listened to a stupid kid. That's what he's doing, Jude. My baby is out there searching for me.' She slapped her hand to her forehead, then wiped her hair from her face. 'Bloody hell, Tommy.'

'Okay, so that's good news, at least.'

'It is?'

'Sure. If he thinks you're on your way to America, then that's where he's heading, which means one thing. He's gone to the ferry. How else would he get off the island?'

They both looked back at the sea, silently praying he didn't try to swim across to the mainland. Their faces met again, and Harriet shook her head.

'He wouldn't, would he, Jude?'

God, I hope not.

'No. He's smart, Harriet. I reckon he's heading for the ferry.'

Harriet seemed to perk up. 'That's good. Queenie will get a hold of him over there.'

'Who is Queenie?'

'Oh, she runs a B&B over by our closest ferry port. Knows all the comings and goings. Trust me, she'll be on it. Let me ring her before I call Mum.'

Jude glanced once more at the angry waves, and for a moment he imagined himself out there, saving people.

That's it. As soon as Tommy is found, I'm heading over to the nearest RNLI station to find this Bert guy. This is where I need to be.

He gestured towards the road, signalling for Harriet, who was still on the phone, to follow him back to the car. He switched on the wipers and the heating. Harriet was shivering, and he wasn't entirely sure if it was her nerves or the dampness setting into her bones from the rain.

Her hand shot out to cover his as she ended the call. 'Mum's calling round to update everyone, and, yes, the RNLI are also on the case. God bless them.' She glanced back at the beach. 'It's not too choppy. I'd be mortified if it were a storm and our Tommy wasn't even out there, which I know he's not, but they're taking no chances. Poxy wetsuit. Of all the things to take with him.'

'My first surfboard was my pride and joy, so I know how he feels. And, just think, when we get him home, and he finds out the truth about you not going anywhere and our new business adventure, he will be over the moon.'

Harriet smiled softly. It was weak, but a smile all the same. 'He will, won't he?'

'Focus on that part, okay, Hal. Everything's gonna be fine.'

'He will love The Old Boat Clubhouse. He'll… Wait, I've thought of somewhere else he might be.'

22

Harriet

Harriet wished Jude would drive faster, but she knew he wanted to get over to the harbour as safely as possible, what with the roads being wet. She noticed his eyes were crinkled in the corners, perhaps from concentrating too much, or maybe because he was also worried about Tommy. He had been by her side since she found out about her son's disappearing act, and she silently thanked Milly for having the idea to make the Isle of Wight the place to help rebrand Keaton Byrd.

Jude inhaled loud enough to be heard over the pitter-patter of the raindrops on the car.

He's been so kind. So helpful. I wonder if he knows how grateful I am for him.

'Thanks, Jude,' she practically whispered, as her voice cracked without warning.

His head briefly turned to glance her way before looking back at the road. 'What for?'

'Being here with me now.'

'Where else would I be?' He almost sounded offended.

Harriet grazed her teeth over her bottom lip. 'It's just, well, I'm not used to having someone by my side. I know I have my family, but, oh, you know what I mean.' She lowered her face to her lap for a second, took a breath, then returned to scanning the streets for Tommy.

Jude's hand met hers on her lap and gave a gentle squeeze of her fingertips. 'We've got plans, you and me. Whatever comes our way, we'll figure it out, together. Okay?'

Harriet's heart lifted. It was nice to hear. Brilliant, in fact, but she wasn't used to that kind of partner. Tommy's dad would fill her with pipe dreams and a fake future. He had his own agenda but strung her along because her feelings mattered little to him. Having Jude, who was the complete opposite, was a dream come true. It was hard to process at times. She suddenly realised she didn't know how to have a normal, loving relationship, because she'd never had one. She gave his hand a gentle squeeze and noticed the crinkles around his eyes were back.

'Can we park by the boats?' he asked, not taking his attention away from the road.

'No, but there's a small car park for the boat club. It won't matter if we park there.' She shrugged, then pointed the way to the entrance.

'Do you really think Tommy will be on board your sister's boat?'

'It's worth a shot. He might be trying to figure out how he can sail it over to the mainland, or America. I did call Lexi, but it went straight to answerphone. She's outside, somewhere, looking for him, but I doubt she'd look on her boat. Why would she?'

'Poor Tommy. He must be distraught.'

'Please, don't. I can't bear the thought of him thinking I would leave him.'

'I feel responsible, Hal.' He parked in an empty space and got out at the same time as her.

She grabbed his hand as he came closer, pulling him towards Lexi's boat. 'No one is to blame, Jude. Kids say stupid things, and Tommy's listened. That's all.' Her powerwalk turned into a sprint as Lady Silver came into view. 'Tommy,' she yelled, tugging Jude. 'Tommy?'

Before they approached the gangplank, a tiny head poked up over the side of the boat, looking dishevelled and a hundred ways lost.

Harriet's heart leapt into her throat. She stopped for all but a second before letting go of Jude's hand and practically vaulting over the safety rail to dive onto the vessel. 'Oh, baby.' She dropped to her knees and flung her arms around him, holding him tighter than she had ever done in his life.

'Mum, I can't breathe,' he managed to mumble.

She pulled back, checking him over for any signs of anything. His dark hair was matted to his forehead and his baby blues were bloodshot and confused. Harriet tightened her lips and poked him lightly in the chest. 'As if I would ever leave you behind, you silly sausage.' She flashed him a warm smile and pulled him in for another hug.

'Digby said you'd gone to America and wasn't coming back,' he mumbled into her top.

Harriet held his shoulders so they were face to face with each other. 'Oh, what does Digby know about anything? He still eats the sand at the beach.'

Tommy giggled, showing his dimples at their deepest.

Jude stepped closer and crouched to their level. He placed his hand over Tommy's hair and smiled. 'So, what was the plan, Captain? Were you about to sail the seas? See the world? Steal your aunt's boat?'

Tommy laughed again, then removed himself from his mum's arms to hug Jude, taking her by surprise. And Jude, it would seem.

Wow! Tommy really likes Jude. Well, what do you know. I don't know what to say now, and I had a whole mouthful for him as well. I'm not interrupting this moment. Not while they're bonding. Oh goodness, what a day! Thank you, Lord, for keeping my son safe, or guardian angel. Whoever.

Whatever. I don't care. Just thank you. Thank you so much. Flipping heck, I can breathe properly again.

She inhaled deeply, filling her lungs, and relaxing her shoulders. Her body felt back to normal, which meant she could now feel the dampness settling into her bones. Tommy had no coat on, so she could only imagine how chilly he might be. Although, knowing him, he wasn't feeling the weather at all. He was always a warm-blooded kid. Still, bath and dinner were needed.

And I better ring Mum to call off the search.

She unlocked her aching legs and walked over to the back of the boat, leaving Jude talking to Tommy about needing a licence to take the boat out.

Fiona answered the call on the first ring. 'Bleeding heck, Harriet. You kids will be the death of me,' was her response to the news. She told her daughter to hurry home and she'd have a hot bath waiting along with fish fingers and chip butties.

Harriet took another lung-filled intake of salty air before turning back to her son and the most gorgeous man she'd ever met.

Jude smiled up at her from his crossed-legged position on the wet decking, and she made a mental note to get an extra key so they could sit inside the next time they were on board Lady Silver. He gestured for her to join them on the floor, so she did, snuggling Tommy into her side.

'Well, Tommy. What do you have to say?' Jude nudged him gently.

Tommy's tired expression went straight to her heart, then her soul, then ended up owning her completely. 'I'm sorry I ran away from school, Mum. I won't do it again.'

'And…' said Jude.

Tommy smiled weakly. 'And I know you wouldn't leave me. I shouldn't have listened to Digby.'

Harriet shook her head slightly. 'No. You shouldn't have, but you've learned a valuable lesson today.'

Tommy frowned. 'What's that?'

Jude grinned and nudged him again. 'That you can't sail a boat without a licence.'

Harriet pursed her lips at Tommy. 'Hmm! Well, I think it's time we went home, don't you?'

Tommy shook his head. 'Jude said we own a water sports shop now. I want to go there.'

Harriet raised her hands to the sky. 'It's raining. We need to get dry, get fed, and get… Hang on a minute.' She glanced at Jude, lowering her hands and raising her eyebrows instead. 'You told him?'

Jude shrugged. 'He needed a happy boost.'

Harriet snorted out a laugh. 'After today, I think we all need a happy boost. My mum needs a week in the Caribbean, and my dad will be needing one or two gulps from his secret stash.'

'And an onion,' said Tommy, making them laugh.

The joy on her boy's face, along with the warm glow coming from Jude, made sitting on a boat in the harbour in the rain seem perfectly normal for all but a moment. The dreary sky, the blustery wind, the salt in the air all became invisible, and a level of tranquillity she had never experienced swept over her soul, taking her to a realm filled with pure love and happiness.

I hope we always feel this complete. I don't want to move. This moment can never end. I've learned my own lesson today. It doesn't matter where we are, as long as we're together. It's us being here creating our own circle that makes everything perfect. And my circle is perfect. My boys are perfect. Oh well, time to go.

She tapped Jude's arm, gesturing for him to stand up with her, but he grabbed her hand and pulled her close, kissing her lips.

Tommy groaned as he stood. 'Yuk!'

Harriet felt Jude's smile on her mouth. 'We need a hot bath,' she mumbled, enjoying feeling his smile widen.

'Sounds great.'

'Is Nan doing fish fingers?' asked Tommy, helping Harriet to her feet.

'Yes, and she's probably going to tell you off for running away. You know that, right?'

Tommy shrugged as he grinned cheekily. 'Nah, she won't. She said my dimples will always stop me being in trouble with anyone. Just smile, she says.'

'Oh, is that right?' Harriet gave Jude a disbelieving look. 'She never let us get away with anything when we were kids.'

Tommy grabbed his bag, containing his beloved wetsuit, and climbed over the rail. 'That's because you haven't got cute dimples, Mum.'

Harriet's hands playfully hit her hips as she huffed out towards him. She went to say something, but Jude's arms hooped through hers, snaking their way around her waist. The warmth from his mouth was on her damp neck, sending a shiver straight down her spine.

'You're cute everywhere,' he whispered onto her skin.

She turned in his arms and gave him a quick peck on the cheek. 'When we get back to mine, I'll show you how cute I can be in the bath.'

His grin warmed every inch of her chilly body instantly. 'I'll hold you to that.'

'Are you moving in with us now?' called out Tommy, picking up a wet stone at the foot of a bench.

Harriet frowned at him as she made her way over. 'Put that down, and no, he—'

'Soon,' interrupted Jude, winking as Harriet glanced back at him.

Ooh, does he mean it? He looks as though he's being serious, even with that goofy wink he gave me. Well, I guess he is settling here, and he's starting up the business, and he wants me and my son in his life. Erm...

'Yes, soon,' she called out to Tommy, without dragging her gaze away from Jude. She took the opportunity to wink back, but just at that moment, the wind shot past her, whipping up a fallen leaf from somewhere that targeted her left eye. She slapped her hand over her face whilst Jude laughed and caught her as she tumbled off the gangplank.

Tommy giggled and pointed her way. 'Mum, are you trying to be a pirate?'

'Ooh arr!' she roared, running up to him to tickle his side. Tommy sprinted away, and Harriet chased him to the car park, leaving Jude to catch them up, which he did in record time. He lifted Tommy into the air and threw him over his shoulder, making the boy squeal with delight, then he leaned over and pulled Harriet into his side and kissed her head.

Harriet glanced up, showing him her smile was coming from deep within her heart.

Jude held a more subdued expression. His eyes narrowed and his lips parted, then he mouthed, 'I love you.'

23

Jude

Tommy had been bathed, put in his pyjamas, and fed more fish fingers than Jude thought possible to eat. He thought he'd be polite about the bathroom situation, but Harriet pulled him inside once she had finished running another hot bath.

The steam and smell of something sweet wrapped around him as he watched Harriet pull out another dark towel from a cupboard.

'Here,' she said, handing it his way. 'I'll turn around while you change.'

Jude smiled to himself as he stripped and tied the towel around his waist.

'The towels are a bit old, I'm afraid,' she mumbled towards the frosted window. 'I might add a new towel bundle to Mum's Christmas list.'

'You can turn around now.'

She did, taking him in from head to toe, which made his eyebrows lift along with the corners of his mouth. She cleared her throat, then glanced at the bath. 'Erm…'

Okay, now she looks awkward. Be a gentleman, Jude. What would your mother say?

He held back his laugh, tightening his brow in an attempt to be serious. 'Shall I wait outside until you're finished, then take my turn?' He waited, watching her mull it over. Her lips were twisted to one side and her nose slightly wrinkled. He grabbed the key in the lock. 'I'll wait in your room.'

'No,' she practically yelled, making herself jump, by the look of things. She took a tentative step towards him, her hand edging his way before relaxing back at her side. She clutched the top of her towel and slowly looked up.

Oh, you'd better tell me to go, Harriet, because you standing there in your towel is all a bit too much for me. My God, you're beautiful.

He went to speak, but she seemed to leap forward, and the next thing he knew, her mouth was on his. It stayed there a moment. Tender. Soft. And Jude's heartbeat rebooted. He pulled her closer and their kiss heated immediately. She leaned into him, causing his feet to shift backwards and his back to land on the door. Harriet had him pinned, but he didn't care.

'Jude, I...' Her voice trailed off, somewhere far away where dreams were made and the softest songs sung.

He slid his hands into her straggly hair, cupping her head and bringing her closer to his body. The heat from her tongue warmed every part of him, causing wave after wave of adrenaline to hit him just as wonderfully as the ones in the ocean. She was his ocean. Her scent, her touch, those beautiful sea-filled eyes that drove him to his knees.

'Harriet.' He pulled her away and took a breath. 'We should cool down.'

'I don't want to. I want you, Jude. I'm ready.'

Oh, baby, I am so ready for you, you would not believe, but how are we supposed to relax in your bathroom with your family downstairs?

Harriet's mouth pressed upon his once more as she stroked over his forearms, tugging him down towards the white lino.

Jude followed her all the way, then slowly unfolded her towel so it flapped open either side of her. He gazed at her bare skin, then raised his eyes to meet hers. 'Harriet, you have an incredible figure, tell me you know that about yourself, right?'

She moistened her lips with her tongue and gave him a grin filled with mischief and desire. 'I swim. A lot.'

Jude bit his bottom lip as he breathed out a laugh. 'Miss Hadley, are you trying to tease me?'

'I'm not teasing. I'm offering.'

'Oh, is that so?'

He watched her struggle to hold in her laugh. She was way too adorable, especially lying naked with him. He had little choice but to kiss her cheeky grin. The feeling of her chest pressed against his brought butterflies to his whole being and a need to take things all the way and even further, if that was possible. He was pretty sure there were places they could explore together, but something was niggling at him. He pulled his face away from hers, then gravitated to her jawline, then her neck, and off to her collarbone.

Get a grip, Jude.

He pulled away.

Harriet's soft fingers slowly stroked over his eyebrow. 'What's wrong?'

'Your family is downstairs. I feel like a teenager.'

Harriet muffled her laugh, then turned her head to kiss his biceps. 'Lose your towel, Jude.'

The words alone caused his stomach to flip, but before his brain had time to process, debate, and come to a logical conclusion, he had pulled the towel from between them.

Just for a moment, time stood still. Harriet was gazing into his eyes, holding a look that told him not to move. His body had already got the memo. He was pretty sure he wasn't going anywhere. But then alarm bells rang, waking him from the hypnotic trance he had with her.

'I don't have any protection on me, Hal.'

Harriet's dreamy expression changed to despondency. 'Oh, I haven't either. And I'm not on the pill. Not that I would mind having more babies. I just think we're—'

'Just getting started. That we need to get our business up and running first, then get a home sorted, and then we can have all the babies you want.' Watching Harriet's face light up warmed his heart.

'Do you want to have children?'

'With you, I want everything. So, yeah, sure, once we're settled. What do you say?'

'I say, we're making a lot of plans lately.'

Jude kissed the edge of her mouth. 'I want you to feel stability with me.' He kissed behind her ear and smiled when it tickled her. 'We have Tommy to think about. Stability is important for kids.' He met her gaze. 'We can take him over to Pepper Bay tomorrow, after school, to check out our new business. Meanwhile, we'll go in the morning and size things up. Sound like another good plan?'

'It does, but what about right now?'

'You want to go now?'

'No. I meant, what are we going to do about the situation we're in?'

Jude grinned widely as he leaned up to scan over her body. He groaned and lowered his head, almost meeting her stomach. 'I guess, the next plan is to bath, then eat. Cold fish fingers, probably. And what the hell is a butty, anyway?'

'Chip sandwich. My grandad used to say a chip butty was his favourite thing to eat.'

Jude lifted himself up to a sitting position. 'Come on, let's get bathed while it's still warm.'

'Ooh, I was relaxed down here as well.'

'Yeah? Do you want to be more relaxed?'

171

Harriet's brow wrinkled along with her nose. 'What do you mean? You know we can't do anything now.'

Jude leaned down and kissed her belly button. 'Wanna bet?' He lowered his mouth, meeting her thigh, then raised his head to smile her way, using his eyes to ask for her permission.

Harriet chewed her bottom lip and blushed, although he wasn't sure if that was from the steam in the room, but he wanted to believe it was from the steam he was offering to produce for her. She nodded and closed her eyes, still smiling, which made him smile way more as he lowered his mouth back to her leg.

24

Harriet

Harriet and Jude stood inside The Old Boat Clubhouse, looking up at the cobwebs high in the corners of the nicotine-stained ceiling. They stayed still for at least a minute, neither of them having much to say about the dust, dirt, cracked walls, and broken floorboards.

Jude sneezed, breaking the silence.

'Bless you.'

'Thank you.' He wiped his nose with a tissue he pulled from his jeans shorts and then waggled it above him. 'At least the roof is waterproof.'

Harriet glanced back at the old door with its rusty hinges. It was still partially open, so she could see the heavy rain falling outside. 'That's good. It's getting worse out there. You know we're due a storm later. Looks like it might come in a bit sooner than expected.'

Jude inspected the ceiling once more. 'Well, I guess it's lasted this long, so should be okay.'

'Oh, this hut has been here for years. We'll visit Grandad tomorrow, and he'll tell you all he knows about the place. I think he was one of the last members.' She moved over to the empty countertop and ran one finger through the thick dust lining its old wood. 'I reckon this could be restored. It's the only original thing in here, so it would be nice to keep it. What do you think?'

Jude closed the door, shutting out the rain. 'There really isn't anything else here, is there?'

'It was storage for the shop for years. Now it's been cleared out, we have space.'

'Space and a counter.'

Harriet put all her weight on top of the slab, pushing down with her arms. 'Seems sturdy.' She smiled as Jude leaned over her back.

'Hmm, guess so.'

She put one hand behind her to tickle his ribs. 'Get off, you big goof.' Jude wriggled away, and she turned to lean against what used to be the bar when the old hut was in full swing.

Jude was checking out a side wall. 'I'm thinking, a plasterer, a carpenter, we can do the paintwork, perhaps lay the flooring. This wall would be good for boards, and over there in the corner, we could create a small changing room, maybe.'

'Sounds good, but first...' Harriet pointed at the large box of cleaning products they had brought with them. 'This place needs a good scrub.'

Jude groaned, making her laugh, then pulled out a yellow duster, eyeing it with compassion. 'I don't hold out much hope for you, my friend.'

Harriet removed it from his grip and gestured to the dirt on the windows. 'Let's clean them first, then wash things down before dusting.'

'Ah, yes. I forgot this is your area of expertise.'

She noticed his pause and could tell he wanted to add more to the conversation. 'What were you about to say?'

He approached the small basin behind the counter and grinned her way when running water came out of the tap. 'I was wondering if you were going to quit your hotel job and work here with me full-time.'

'Well, I think I should keep it, for now. It's only the morning shift, and the money might come in handy.'

'Keaton's money will help us.'

I forgot about that. How strange to suddenly have money sitting in my bank account. What if I use it all and end up with nothing? What if someone steals it from my account? What if I die before I get a chance to spend it? Oh, flipping heck, why is having money such a worry? I never had to worry about that stuff before.

'Jude, should we have a money plan?'

He sneezed again and wiped his nose. 'Hmm? What do you mean?'

'Well, between us, we have all this money. Should we divvy it up? Put sections of it into different areas?'

He gave a non-committal shrug and started to fill a bucket with water. 'Sure, if you want.'

'I think we need a budget. One for this place, another for our future home, one for a rainy day.'

Jude raised his hands. 'Like right now.'

'You know what I mean. We need to make sure we don't drink it all up. We have to have some left over in case we have days where we don't earn much. We need—'

'Whoa, whoa, whoa. Slow down, babe.' He turned off the tap and faced her. 'We're not gonna run out of money, okay.'

'You don't know that.'

'Erm, yeah, I do.'

'Jude, you're not being very realistic.'

'Hal, you're being pessimistic.'

'Am not.'

'Are too.'

Harriet huffed, slapping the duster to her hip. 'Jude Jackson, were you born with a silver spoon in your mouth? Is that why you don't money-worry?'

175

'Money-worry? Erm, yes and no.'

'What?'

'Yes, I was born with a rather nice spoon in my mouth. Not entirely silver, but pretty decent all the same. No, I don't worry about money. I've never had to, but that doesn't make me stupid when it comes to the stuff. I know how to budget. I know how to pay my bills. And I happen to know we're gonna be all right.'

Blimming heck. He doesn't get it at all. He might be used to not worrying about money running out, but I am. How am I supposed to explain that to Mr Laid-back over there?

Jude dried his hands on a cloth and waved her over as he took a step forward. She snuggled into his top, inhaling his usual scent mixed with dust. 'Harriet, I don't want you to worry about money, okay. I've got it covered.'

She lifted her face up to meet his narrowed eyes and cheeky grin. 'I want to help too, you know. And I can't help but worry about money. It's my default.'

Jude kissed the headscarf holding back her hair and pulled her in for a tighter hug. 'We're gonna be okay. But it's up to you if you want to keep working at the hotel for a while until you feel more financially comfortable.' He moved her back and raised her chin. 'Hey, this is about us as the family we're becoming. We're a team now, and we're gonna do whatever's right for all of us. Just know, one day, you will feel secure with me, the business, our home, money, the whole lot. I'll spend every day making sure you feel stable at all times.'

Harriet couldn't help but smile at him as her whole being filled with warmth. 'You're sweet, do you know that?'

'Aww, I know.' He kissed her before she could laugh or speak.

She couldn't believe how much her life had changed. All those years, day in day out, the same old life passing her by, occupied by Tommy and swimming.

And now this. Him. Hollywood film stars, fat lumps of cash, new business. New beginnings. I don't think it's possible to feel any happier. I can't keep thinking it's all going to disappear any moment. Oh, why must I be such a worrywart?

She stared up at him to see him smiling her way.

'Harriet, I could kiss you for a hundred years and never get bored.'

The heat coming from every part of him had Harriet melting into the dusty floorboards, and that's exactly where she took him. Jude laughed on her lips as they met the dust and hard wood.

'I want to kiss you forever, Jude.'

A bang of thunder filled the air, causing them both to jump.

'Jeez, is this your summertime?'

'Pretty much. Sun, mini-heatwave, storm. Welcome to Britain.'

'At least it's still warm.' Jude nudged her nose with his own as she flipped him onto his back. 'So, I'm trapped in an old cabin on a small island in the middle of a storm. Hmm, whatever can I do to pass the time? What do the Brits do?' He waggled his eyebrows, making her laugh.

'Play cards.'

'You want to play poker?'

'Have you ever played strip poker?'

Jude's smile almost filled his face. 'We haven't got any cards, but we can still manage the strip part, I reckon.'

Harriet was two steps ahead of him. Her fingers fumbled around the top three buttons on his top, with more urgency than she had anticipated. She stopped and giggled to herself.

'Oh, no, don't stop now, Harriet. It's all coming off. Mine. Yours.' He glanced sideways. 'We're gonna need the towel for the floor. You do pick your moments.'

Harriet sat up to straddle him. 'By any chance, have you got any protection on you today?'

Jude tried to pull his wallet out of his back pocket whilst she was still sitting on him. 'Hell yeah.'

Harriet stood, giving him room to move. A flash of lightning lit up the window as the rain bashed hard against the pane. She peered outside at the gloomy sky, then at the waves bashing against some rocks below. Jude's hands snaked around her waist, and his chin rested on her head.

'Do you like storms, Hal?'

'Love them. How about you?'

'Yeah, they're pretty cool. When you're not out there. You know, once I'm settled, I'm going to volunteer for the RNLI.'

She spun around in his arms. 'Flipping heck, Jude. They go out to save people in bad weather like this. I don't know what it's like where you live, but over here, we have people who go close to the sea during a storm, for all different reasons. Some take pictures, others want to get a buzz. People take their kids, would you believe? And we have some who walk their dogs. It's all go, you know.' She tapped her chest in annoyance. 'It's our rescue teams that have to risk their own lives to go out saving those idiots. You need to think about that. It's one thing to save someone who is in trouble, thanks to a rip or something, but to risk your life for someone who was being reckless, well, Jude, I'm not sure how I feel about you doing that.'

He kissed her forehead and then trailed his mouth along her neck. 'You can come to the open day the station is having in a few weeks. Check it out for yourself. I'll be okay. You'll see.'

I won't see. It's not the same as surfing the largest wave, Jude. Oh God, he's an adrenaline junkie, isn't he? I bet he would love to be on a boat in a storm. Blooming nutcase. Great! This is my new worry. No doubt, Tommy will grow up wanting to be just like him.

'Hey, stop worrying about things that haven't happened, Hal. Instead, how about focusing on the here and now.'

'Well, right now, we need to fix this place up, and—'

Jude's mouth was back on hers, and his hands were in her hair, sliding back the red headscarf, and Harriet could do little else but remove his top, because it had been bugging her all day anyway.

She felt her weight lighten as Jude lifted her over to the counter, where he sat her upon the dark towel he'd quickly slid beneath her. Harriet wrapped her legs around him, holding him close. She didn't know where to touch first. Every part of his body was calling her, and she felt overwhelmed for a moment.

The idea of making love to Jude had entered her dreams every night since the day she laid eyes on him in the lift at the hotel. He smelled like the sea and the sand. The minute he touched her, she entered a world where nothing would ever be right without him.

'I love you, Jude,' she whispered close to his ear.

His hands slid into her hair, causing a swirl of thin strands to cascade out of two clips. His mouth lined her neck, and she momentarily stopped him so she could remove her top. Jude's lips quickly returned to her skin, causing her butterflies to surf the waves rolling over and over her heart.

The thunder rumbled loudly, swiftly followed by a flash of lightning, and Harriet noticed Jude checking the window. She leaned back on the counter, waiting for his face to return to her.

'I think we're stuck in here for a while, Jude.'

'Yeah, I…' His breath caught as he turned back her way, and immediately his hands were on her waist, pulling her into him.

Harriet reached down to undo her shorts, and Jude quickly helped whilst kissing her stomach. Before she had time to stretch her arms all the way over her head, her bottoms had been removed, and she felt more exposed than ever before. Her head lifted slightly to glance at the door.

God, I hope no one comes in. I doubt they will, but still. I would die a thousand deaths if someone saw me like this.

As though reading her mind, Jude went over to the door and turned the key. 'Better?' he asked on his return.

She smiled and relaxed back as much as she could on the old counter. Whilst she waited for Jude to lose his bottoms, she arched her back, trying for sexy and seductive, hoping it would make him hurry back to her. It did, which was good, because her back was starting to ache. The hard wood wasn't helping, and she was struggling to hold back a sneeze.

'Achoo!'

Oh my God, I sneezed in his face.

Jude pulled in his lips as he wiped one hand down his cheek. 'I would say bless you, but I'm still absorbing your germs.'

Harriet burst out laughing, trying hard to apologise in between breaths.

Jude leaned over and pulled her up to a sitting position. She flopped on his shoulder, giggling into his neck until he moved them closer together. 'You okay, Hal?' His voice was low and had a slight catch to each word.

Her stomach flipped as he joined their bodies for the first time. 'Yes,' she managed, not wanting to speak at all.

'Oh, Hal. I don't want to move. I want this moment to last forever.'

'Me too,' she whispered, then arched her back again, drawing him closer whilst breathing out his name, knowing full well there was no way Jude was going to stay still any longer.

25

Jude

The storm had settled a touch and the rain was calm. Most of the cleaning had been done, and Jude was trying to fix a broken floorboard that looked quite dangerous if trod on. Something caught his eye beneath the floor and dust, so he wriggled his fingers between the sharp crack, edging towards the tinny item.

What is that? Why won't it budge? If I can just...

'Ow!' He pulled back his hand to look at the giant splinter poking out near his little finger.

'You okay down there, Jude?' Harriet quickly joined him on the floor, taking his wounded hand in hers.

'Ow!' he yelped again, as Harriet plucked out the splinter in one quick swipe.

'There, that wasn't so bad.' She kissed his knuckles and smiled sweetly.

Jude ignored her charm and examined his sore instead. 'We need to buy a first aid kit for in here.'

'I'll put it on our to-do list. Meanwhile, what were you doing sticking your hand under the floorboards? Goodness knows what's lurking down there.'

Jude pointed at the tin box he could now see quite clearly. 'Trying to get that.'

Harriet slipped her slim hand into the small hole, wriggled about a bit, then removed the item from its prison. 'Ooh, it's so dirty.' She lifted it closer to her nose. 'And it pongs a bit.'

Jude lowered her arm. 'Take it away from your face. It could have been down there since the Black Death.'

She laughed and waved it his way, making him lean back.

'Hal, stop.' He breathed out a laugh and got her to place the old box on the floor in front of them. 'I want to know what's inside, but I'm thinking a severed finger might put me off my lunch.'

Harriet leaned into his arm, nudging him playfully. 'It's not going to be someone's finger.'

'So why does it smell so bad?'

'Probably because it's been stuck underground for so long. It does look quite old, or maybe the dampness down there caused the rust, making it look older than it is. We'll need to have someone look at our foundations before we sort the flooring. Best to be safe.'

'Yeah, okay. Add that to the list.' Jude reached out for the box. 'With a bit of luck, there'll be some treasure, which can pay for the repairs around here.'

'Ooh, pirate treasure.'

Jude's eyes widened. 'Did you really have pirates here?'

'This is England. We had pirates everywhere. Anyway, pirates like to travel. They probably visited the world and its sister.'

'Do you think this could have been a place for smugglers?'

'Doubt it. They liked coves and secret hideaways. You can see this place from the water.'

Jude took a breath, mostly because the tin box wafted its slight stench his way, and then he attempted to remove the lid. 'It's stuck.'

'Here, try this.' Harriet handed him a screwdriver.

'Did we bring this?'

'I found it under the sink. Try it. Wedge it underneath.'

Jude jiggled the tool and the tin whilst Harriet flapped her hands above his, obviously worrying he might slip and lose a finger. 'Hal, move your hands, I can't… Oh, look. It's open.'

They both peered down as Jude removed the rusty lid. Inside, was a small bundle of letters, and as he took them out, a golden key was sitting on the bottom.

Harriet held the key in the palm of her hand. Holding it up to the light. 'If this is real gold, then that's the treasure, but I doubt it is.' She gestured at the letters. 'See if there's a treasure map in there.'

'I've always wanted to go on a treasure hunt. I went diving once to look at a shipwreck, but there was nothing down there except the souls of sailors.'

Harriet gave him a look. 'Oh, well, that's cheerful.'

Jude shrugged as he pulled out the top letter from the thin-thread rope holding them together. 'There's nothing on the envelope.' He opened the tea-stained-looking paper to read the cursive words written in dark ink.

Harriet nudged his arm, then leaned closer. 'Read it out loud, Jude.'

'Okay, it's to someone called Dusty. It says I wish we could be here together at the same time. It's killing me we have to hide. I hate this. All the chaos, the secrets, the lies. I love you so much, and I want to live my life with you. Why can't we have that? It's not fair. Please, run away with me. Let's just go. Make a plan with me, Dusty. Let's sail away. I want to fall asleep in your arms and wake each morning with you by my side. All I see is your beautiful face. Those aquamarine eyes that warm my soul. You're mine, Dusty Renshaw, and I'll always be yours. Lost in you always, Conway.'

Harriet held one hand over her heart. 'Oh, that's so lovely, and a little sad. I'm not sure how I feel.'

'Seems as though this might have been a love nest at some point.' He scanned over the letter. 'There's no date.'

'Look, the next one has a C on the front. Read that one. It might be from Dusty.'

Jude carefully placed the letter by his side, afraid it might crumble in his hands if he moved too fast. He slid the next one out of the string. 'We could find out who these belong to and hand them over. Might be someone's family around here.'

Harriet's brow crinkled as she faced him. 'Not sure I know those names, but there is a Renshaw family in Pepper Bay. They own a hotel called Pepper River Inn. Could be their relative. See what the next one says.'

'My dearest Conway. You know how I feel about you. Meet me here at dawn on Tuesday. I'll say I'm taking an early morning swim. I can't wait to hold you. I want to kiss you all over. I miss you so much, it actually burns me. I wish things could be different for us, but you know I can't change this world. But I'll change our lives. We'll find a way to live how we want. To be together. Forever. I love you, Con. Lost in you always. D.'

'Oh my goodness. This is so romantic.' Harriet scrunched her top in her fingertips. 'I feel a bit emotional now.'

'Hey, come here.' Jude kissed her head, staying with his mouth pressed against her hair for a moment.

Man, I know how this person feels. If it's half of what I feel for this lady, then I'm with them all the way. But what's stopping this couple from being together?

'Do you think they were having an affair, Hal?'

'I don't know. It's a bit odd, and I wonder what this key has to do with anything.' She held it back up for them both to ponder over. 'Let's read them all, Jude. I know it's intrusive, but I want to uncover the mystery.' She breathed

185

out a long sigh and leaned back into his side. 'Who knew this place would hold secrets. I've only ever known it to hold rolls of material.'

Jude laughed quietly as he opened the next letter. 'Conway wrote this one. Being in the water with you, so far out to sea, where we are free, are the most exhilarating moments in my life. To feel you. To touch you. Have your bare skin upon mine. Taste every part of you. I can't get our night together out of my head. Oh, how I thank that storm for keeping us trapped here. Each time I close my eyes, I feel you. I want to do that with you every day. Dusty, we have to leave here. I cannot stand another moment without you. I feel I'll die soon. Lost in you always. Con.'

Harriet's shoulders drooped along with Jude's. 'Oh, they're killing me, Jude. Do you think they got their happily ever after? I hope so. They seem so in love.'

He winked her way, then leaned in for a kiss. 'I know how they feel.'

'At least we're not hiding from anyone.'

'Anymore. Do you know how hard it was for me seeing you on Keaton's arm? Having the world think you're his girl? Jeez, Harriet, I struggled some days.'

She gently stroked his face, brushing back his sun-kissed hair and smiling into his light-brown eyes. 'It was hard for me too. And I'm so happy I'm your girlfriend. I might even start calling you my old man, if you're lucky.'

Jude laughed as she swung her arms around his neck and hugged him tightly. 'I love you too.'

Harriet slid back to his side and raised his hand to kiss his fingertips. A gesture he happily returned. 'Oh, Jude, I'm so glad we don't have any more worries. No more hiding. No more pretending. No more wondering about each other. Do you think we've rushed things though?'

186

'I don't care about timing. All I know is what feels right. I'm happy. You're happy. Tommy's happy. That's all that matters. We have a plan. We're gonna work on it together, so, as far as I'm concerned, I don't know what happened here in the past, but we certainly got our happily ever after.'

Harriet beamed, making him come alive inside. 'I love us, Jude Jackson.'

'So do I, Harriet Hadley, who will one day be Harriet Jackson, because that's also on the to-do list.'

Harriet gently squeezed his arm. 'I love our to-do list.'

'Me too, honey.'

'Come on, Jude. I want our mystery couple to have a happy ending. We have to read them all. Please, please, let them be together.'

Jude read on, finding more and more love letters, pretty much all saying the same thing. Two people loving each other, but something was keeping them apart. Nothing was added to their story by the last letter, so they didn't find out how the romance ended. 'Well, that was an anti-climax.'

'We're seeing Grandad tomorrow. We'll ask him if he knew these people. We'll do that before going up to Pepper River Inn. I'm a bit worried these letters might upset someone. What if it was an affair and the family still don't know about it? I don't want to be the one who delivers the news.'

26

Harriet

The Wilson-Holmes Retirement Village wasn't as quiet and calm as it usually was, as Harriet and Jude discovered as they entered the foyer. An old lady was clinging to a bottle of cherryade as though her life depended on it, and the exhausted care worker was desperately trying to keep a good grip of the top half himself.

Harriet raised her hand to her mouth to muffle her giggle whilst Jude looked confused.

A man in his nineties was waving his walking stick in the air, trying to gain the cherryade hoarder's attention, which only caused him to slip, then slide down the doorframe that softened his fall. A young carer rushed to his aid whilst another lady was shouting at a dark-haired woman who was leaving the building, telling her not to come back.

'Is it normally this rowdy in here?' whispered Jude.

Harriet went to reply but frowned angrily when the leaving woman barged into her shoulder as she passed her by. 'Er, excuse me.'

The dark-haired lady ignored her and stormed off.

'Cheek of her.' Harriet scoffed and looked down as Jude curled his fingers around hers. She leaned closer to him and gestured over to the large bottle of cherryade. 'That's old Dolly. She used to own Dolly's Haberdashery, which means—'

'She owned The Old Boat Clubhouse too,' whispered Jude.

The struggle was still going on, and Harriet had to admire the old woman's strength.

I should help. She might not remember me, but it could be nice for her to have someone step in. That care worker looks as though he would appreciate any help.

'Jude, give me a sec.' Harriet tentatively approached the argument. 'Hello, Dolly. Do you remember me? I'm Harriet Hadley. Fiona's daughter. My grandfather is a resident here too. Stu Sharpe.'

Dolly grumbled something as she loosened her hold on her drink, but not enough for the carer to take it away. 'I know your family. Can you help me, my lovely? This thieving bugger won't let go of my cherryade.'

A long sigh came from the carer, directed at Harriet. 'She's only allowed a small amount each day.' He grimaced at Dolly. 'And she knows the rules.'

'Oh, rules schmules. Don't tell me what to do, boy. I've changed your nappy.' Dolly gave one hefty tug of the bottle, catching the man off guard for a moment. She smiled triumphantly and almost fell over as she raised her prized possession in the air as though it were a trophy.

Harriet quickly caught her and steadied the woman before the carer had a chance. 'Now, let me see. How about a compromise. Let's pour a shot of cherryade out for you to have now, then we can put the rest away in the fridge, so it'll keep nice and cool, ready for your full glass tomorrow.'

More grumbling noises came from Dolly, followed by a twisting of the lips and further wrinkling of the brow. She sniffed, mulled over her options, then reluctantly agreed, much to the instant relief of the care worker.

'Thank you,' he mouthed, leading Dolly to the kitchen.

Harriet smiled as she walked back over to Jude, who quirked an eyebrow in admiration.

'That was impressive, Hal. Perhaps you should get a job here.'

'Leave off. It's hard work and less pay.' She looped her arm through his and guided him along a hallway. 'Come on, let's go see what Grandad is up to. I can't wait for you to meet him.'

They strolled along the auburn carpet, inhaling the sweet scent of lilies filling the air. The garden could be seen through the large windows along one side of the corridor, revealing the sunlight fighting its way through the fluffy white clouds. A fresh breeze blew in through the opened tops, cooling the warm temperature of the home a touch.

Jude stopped to glance at the pond in the near distance. 'This is a nice place. How long has your grandfather been in here?'

'A few years. He's ninety-one now and still fully with it. It's his body letting him down, which is such a shame. Mum was looking after him for a long while, but it got too much for her. She still feels guilty to this day. She had to sell his house to afford this place, which Grandad wasn't pleased about. Not only were all his memories with his wife there, he wanted to leave Mum the house as her inheritance, but it's all wrapped up in this place.'

'It's a tough decision. My grandmother refused to leave hospital at one point because she was afraid she was going to be moved to a care home, but my dad had full-time carers at her home instead, which was hard. She had dementia, you see. My dad would come home in such a state sometimes after seeing her. It was so sad for everyone.'

Harriet snuggled into him, feeling a tad blessed her grandad could understand what was going on. 'I hope if we ever end up in a home, we come in together.'

'I hope we have that many years together.'

Harriet's lip wobbled, so she quickly pressed her face into his shirt. 'Goodness, I feel all emotional now.' She smiled softly as his arms cradled her, but it didn't stop her from worrying about a life where they would be separated and have to fight for their cherryade.

Jude raised her chin and kissed the tip of her nose. 'Let's concentrate on today. Now, what door number is your grandfather's? Stu, right?'

Pulling herself together, Harriet nodded towards a light wooden door three doors down. 'This way.'

A high-back chair was the first thing that came into view as the door to Stu's room was opened. Beige curtains flanked a square window, almost matching the colour of the thin carpet. A TV was on, showing a gardening programme, and in the orthopaedic bed opposite was Harriet's grandad, sitting up, looking refreshed and happy.

'Hi, Grandad.' She rushed towards his toothless smile, gently hugging his frail body. Leaning back to take him in, Harriet beamed. 'Look at you with your suntan.'

'We've had a lovely summer, apart from that storm. I've been in the garden most days. The bees are loving my geranium patch.'

Harriet looked back at Jude. 'Grandad got the local gardener to plant more flowers for the bees.' She pulled over a comfy brown chair close to the top end of the bed, gesturing for Jude to sit there. 'Grandad, I want you to meet someone.'

Jude stepped around to her side and reached out his hand, which Stu slowly took. 'It's so good to meet you, Stu.'

'And who might you be, young man?'

'He's my boyfriend, Grandad. Jude Jackson.'

Stu's beady eyes peered at Jude. 'He has an accent.'

Harriet smiled whilst she perched at the side of the bed. 'He's American.'

Stu perked up even more. 'Ooh, what brings you here?'

Oh, that's a long story. Where to start? I'm not sure Grandad will understand much. Hmm, let's see…

'Work, Grandad, but now he's staying. He's bought The Old Boat Clubhouse, and we're going to turn it into a water sports shop.'

Stu gently tapped her hand. 'My little water baby.'

Whenever her grandad warmly smiled her way, it always melted her heart that little bit more. He was one of her favourite people in the whole world, filled with magic and mystery, love and laughter, sunshine and the sea.

'Grandad used to swim with me when I was Tommy's age,' she told Jude, who smiled her way.

'That's why I'm still here today, Jude. If you keep fit when you're young, it helps when you're old. You mark my words. Only, you can't go on forever.'

Harriet nodded. 'Grandad only got old when he turned eighty-seven. He was as fit as a butcher's dog before that.'

'You can't outrun the Grim Reaper forever,' said Stu, looking at Jude. 'He'll always be the last one standing.'

Harriet lifted her grandfather's bony fingers to kiss his soft hand. 'Well, right now, you're winning the race, Grandad, and that's all that matters.' She carefully placed his hand back on his lap. 'Now, how are you getting on?'

'Mustn't grumble.' His favourite saying, and one Harriet knew was coming. 'But, tell me about your new adventure. The Old Boat Clubhouse, eh? It's not been much except storage for years.'

Harriet and Jude shared a look before she turned back to face her grandad. 'I was hoping you might have its backstory. There are a few tall tales about the old place.'

Stu chuckled out a raspy laugh. 'I know. People have the wildest imaginations. It was an old meeting ground for men, that's all. Started off with sailors, then turned into a bit of a drinking hole, then it was a swimming club for a while. I used to go. See, nothing much to tell. No skeletons hanging in the closet.'

Harriet shifted on the bed. 'We found some old letters in a tin wedged beneath the floorboards. Grandad, they were love letters between a couple who for some reason couldn't be together. It was a bit sad reading them, and it felt wrong, but we wanted to find out whose family they belonged to. I was thinking of the Renshaws up at Pepper River Inn, because one of the writers was called Dusty Renshaw. Have you heard of her?'

Stu's eyes widened along with his smile. 'Yes, I knew Dusty, but he was a man. Not a woman.'

'Oh, I assumed Dusty was female.' Harriet glanced at Jude. 'You know, like Dusty Springfield. That's who I thought of when I first saw the name. Mum loves her songs.'

Stu coughed, clearing his rattling airwaves, and Jude handed him a plastic beaker from the bedside cabinet. Harriet helped her grandfather sip the water, then dried the corners of his mouth with a tissue from her cardigan pocket.

'So, was Dusty related to the hotel owners?' asked Jude, as Stu settled back into his plump pillows.

'Yes. He used to own the inn along with Conway Trent. They were best friends,' Stu told them, smiling at his old memories.

Well, that explains that. Not sure if I should tell Grandad the other person writing the letters was Conway. This isn't my secret to share. I don't know what to do with these letters now. Maybe I should put them back.

Stu sniffed and wiped his nose using Harriet's tissue. 'I always felt sorry for Dusty and Con. There were rumours back then that they were more than friends. There was a big falling out. The hotel was split in two, and the families stopped talking to each other. Shame. I always liked them. Complete opposites, they were. Dusty all fiery and confident. Conway was the gentle type, you know. Softly spoken. Nice man. They should have been a couple, but that's just my opinion. Life was different back then. We were all expected to get a wife, have kids, and not ask for much more than a steady job and food on the table.'

'Didn't you have any dreams, Grandad?'

'Ooh, yeah. I had one big one. And it came true.'

Jude leaned forward, resting his elbows on his knees. 'What was your dream, Stu?'

'To marry my Patricia. The moment I laid eyes on her, I knew she was all I needed in my life.' His eyes started to water. 'To love someone and be loved back is the best feeling in the world. And love is the most powerful force. I wouldn't change my past for all the tea in China. Your gran was the best thing that happened to me. I've had a blessed life, thanks to her. The only thing I'm sorry about is that she went before me, but she always said she hoped she would. Reckoned I was the stronger one, but I'm not. Kills me every day that she's not here.'

Don't cry, Hal. Keep it together for Grandad. Oh, I think I might have to go before Jude. He'd be able to cope better than me. I feel a right mess thinking about it.

Jude's hand covered hers, and she could tell he was reading her mind.

'So,' added Stu. 'You spend your time enjoying each other, do you hear? Life whizzes by, so you must make those memories count. Every single one. You love each other, make each other a priority, look after each other's hearts, and work as a team. Always. That's how it's done.'

Harriet smiled softly at Jude, then back at her grandad. 'Jude's my teammate, Grandad.' She felt the light squeeze of her hand from Jude's.

27

Jude

A few weeks had passed by, and Jude had been busy in The Old Boat Clubhouse with repairs and paintwork. The owner, Dolly Lynch, agreed to a quick sale, seeing as Jude was a cash buyer. It was so much easier having his mother's assistant interacting with a local solicitor. He didn't want to admit it, but he was pleased for once his mother was taking charge in certain areas. Plus, Harriet didn't seem to mind. He wasn't too sure what she would think of him allowing his parents to get involved, but she assured him she was glad of the help.

Jude glanced around at his business coming together. Tessie from the farm shop was painting one wall whilst Harriet painted another, and the old lady who he met in the tea shop had just left, leaving behind the smell of burnt sage from where she had smudged the place, informing him it would clear the air. He wasn't entirely sure what she had done, but he let her get on with it, as it seemed to make her happy.

He stepped outside to inhale the warm salty air for a moment and found himself gravitating towards the shoreline. The sea was calm as it rolled onto the shingles, creating white foam and a gentle whooshing sound that soothed his soul immediately.

If there was one thing in the world that could own his soul, it was the sea. He longed to be out there, riding a wave or floating on his back. He didn't care what he was doing in the water, as long as he was out there.

He would buy a boat as soon as he had his visa. Cynthia had said it should be this week. He had no idea how she managed to speed it along, but he wasn't complaining. He'd have to send her some flowers or something to say thank you for all her help. She'd been a lifesaver.

He'd never felt so much gratitude before. He had always taken his parents for granted, not giving them the credit they deserved. His mother had been a hundred percent involved. She got Cynthia on the case, giving him everything he needed.

I'm so lucky. Wow, it's taken me to age twenty-seven to realise how blessed I am. Kind of feel like a jerk now.

A hand slid onto his shoulder, bringing him out of his thoughts.

'Hey, Jude. You enjoying the view?' asked Harriet quietly, as though not to disturb him too much.

He turned to wrap his arms around her and kiss her paint-smudged forehead. 'It's a lot better now I'm looking at you.'

She giggled into his top and shifted her head to smile his way. 'The counter has come up a treat since Heath sanded and varnished it. To be honest, I thought he would chuck it out as soon as he saw it, but he said it was worth restoring. I'll have to take you up to Silver Wish Farm one day. You'll love his workshop. Wish I could carve things out of wood. He makes it look so easy.'

'Yeah, all the workers we've had here are so skilled, makes me feel a bit boring. Hey, did you know Heath is a volunteer for the RNLI? And both his brothers. He gave me his brother's number. He's called Finn. He's part of the open day this Saturday. Are you gonna come over there with me to check it out?'

Harriet groaned but remained smiling. 'I guess. I don't want to stop you from doing this, Jude. It's just scary you want to join the boat crew. You know, you could work in one of the shops instead.'

A strand of her hair blew into his mouth as he laughed. 'Nice try, but my heart's already in this.'

'Well, okay. Let's check out what they have to say first.'

Jude turned her around so they were facing the old hut that no longer looked in need of repair. 'I was thinking, what about if we buy something to put at the side there? There's room for a small storage unit. It could hold more equipment.'

'Yeah, looks good. You know, we can actually open soon. Tessie's set us up a website, and I've got some flyers ready to stick through everyone's letterboxes. We'll go over to the caravan parks as well and see if we can advertise on their noticeboards. I feel a bit weird about going over to Pepper River Inn to ask. I still haven't given over the letters. What if it upsets them? They've only just rebuilt their hotel and rebranded. The two families are no longer at war. Married to each other, in fact, but still. It's a worry. I don't want to be the one who puts a spanner in the works.'

'Look, Hal. Just hand them over. It's their family's business, not ours. We'd want to know some history if it were us. It's not our decision to make. I know we found the letters, but it's time to pass them on.'

'Okay. As soon as we get an opening date for this place I'll pop it on our leaflets and head out to distribute them all over the island, then I'll sort that at the same time I'm up there.'

Jude kissed her cheek, feeling so complete having her in his arms. Her grandfather's words had settled deep within him ever since Stu told them how important it was to be a team. Harriet was the only team player he needed.

'Tessie will be leaving soon. So, how about we grab some food from the pub up the road and bring it back here to eat?'

Harriet nodded. 'Ooh, definitely. I'm hungry now you've said that. We should offer to feed Tess too, even though she doesn't have to pay for her food from there, seeing how her parents own The Ugly Duckling.'

'I offered earlier, but she said she had to get home. So, it's just you and me and the big fat surprise I have waiting for you.' He roared out a mischievous laugh, gaining him a nudge in the ribs.

'You can't do that to me. It's not fair. I—'

Tessie called out from the doorway, interrupting them. 'I'm off now. I'll see you tomorrow.'

Jude jogged towards her whilst waving one hand. 'Tess, wait. I want to thank you once again for all your help. You're such a star.'

Tessie flapped her hand at him. 'Oh, leave off. I'm just being a mate. Besides, you'll see soon enough, it's what we do around here. Pepper Bay stick together, and you're one of us now. You had better get looking for somewhere to live around here.' She playfully waggled one finger at Harriet as she approached. 'You don't want to end up on the Sandly side.'

'Oi! Blooming cheek.' Harriet laughed.

Tessie's green eyes widened as her face came alive with excitement. 'Ooh, if you're interested, the Jameson family are about to sell part of their land. They're trying to build up some cash for a holiday villa in Spain, so the rumours go. Anyway, not a bad plot. Worth checking out, I say. You could build a little cottage right up there along Pepper Lane. Don't waste time though. These things get swiped up around here before they're even put down.'

Jude caught the sparkle in Harriet's eyes, telling him she was extremely interested in the idea. He thanked Tessie once again and followed her out to the road, where they all walked uphill to The Ugly Duckling. As soon as Tessie had gone behind the bar to talk to her dad, Jude pulled Harriet over to the unlit fireplace by the back door.

'Oh, Jude, can you read my mind?'

'You want a house around here?'

'Are you kidding? It would be a dream come true to own a cottage along Pepper Lane. They are so sought after. They hardly ever come up for sale. Our Grace has one. Waterside Cottage. Only because her husband bought it from his aunt.' She quietly clapped in front of her chest. 'Oh, Jude, we have to try. Do you think we can afford it? I don't even know how much it costs to build from scratch.'

'We'll do it, if that's what you want. It shouldn't be a problem.'

'Flipping heck, Jude. Do you have your own money printing machine or something?'

He laughed and gestured towards a table so they could sit and check out the menu. 'It's doable, that's all.'

'But we don't have any prices yet. And don't say it doesn't matter.'

He couldn't help but shrug. 'It kind of doesn't. Look, Hal, my money has set up our business. Your money is sitting in the pot for a rainy day to help make you feel settled, and my mother has given me the money for my home back in Malibu. That's what we'll use to buy the land and build whatever home you want.'

'Wow, just like that.'

Jude frowned at the menu. 'Does England have fish and chips on every menu? I swear I haven't seen one yet where it's not included.'

Harriet grabbed his wrist, lowering the menu back to the wooden table. 'Never mind fish and chips. We're making big decisions here.'

'Yeah, what to eat.' He stopped smiling when he saw she had her worry face on. 'Okay. Here's what we'll do. I'll go ask Tessie to call the owner... Jameson family, was it? Well, whoever, and I'll set up a meeting with them. You can get all your figures, then I'll give them the money, and you can get designing.'

Harriet leaned back on her chair and folded her arms. 'Jude, don't make it sound so easy.'

'Harriet, don't add complications where there aren't any.'

She huffed, then unclenched her fists. 'Fair point. Everything's moving really fast, don't you think?'

'We'll have time to slow things down once everything is sorted. It'll take a good while to build a house. We're only at the beginning of our journey together.'

'Really? Because I feel as though we've been together for ten years already.'

Jude laughed and lifted her hand to his mouth. 'In ten years, we're gonna look back at this moment and be so glad we didn't let this opportunity slip through our fingers. So, my love, my teammate, my destiny, do you want me to tell Tessie to make the call?' Watching Harriet's face relax and smile gave him his answer before she even spoke. He stood quickly, kissing her cheek for good measure.

'And order some fish and chips while you're at the bar. Tell Elaine we're taking it away.'

'Yes, ma'am.' He saluted her, then called over to Tessie as she was heading for the door. Once everything was sorted with her, and he had organised a meet-and-greet the next morning over at the Jameson property, he collected his food order and headed back to The Old Boat Clubhouse with Harriet, who had ripped open the foil covering the top plate and was snaffling chips, feeding him as well along the way.

'Oh, Jude,' she said, mouthful. 'I really love my life right now.'

'Me too, honey.'

'Are you going to tell me what my surprise is yet?'

'I thought you'd forgotten, what with the house business going on.'

'Never.' She stuffed another chip in her mouth and grinned. 'I think I've guessed it anyway.'

'Oh, go on then.'

'You're going to let me rename the business.'

Jude stopped walking at the bottom of the slope of Pepper Lane. 'Ah, no, Hal. I like The Old Boat Clubhouse. I even like the ghost sign. It seems a shame to have that artist guy, Scott, paint over it.'

'To be honest, I'm not fussed either way. If you want to keep the name, we'll keep the name, but that means I get to name our new cottage.'

'Ha! Now, you're finally getting on board with positive future thinking. So, what you got in mind?'

'I like coral.'

'Coral?'

'It sounds cute.'

'Coral Cottage. We won't have a sea view, but we do have the shop for that.'

Harriet shrugged and snaffled more chips. 'Ooh, needs more salt.'

Jude pulled her around to their shop. 'You need to sit down and hand over the bottom plate before mine gets cold.' He followed her inside, where they flopped to a white sheet on the floor and continued to eat their dinner.

Harriet waggled a long chip in the air. 'If you have dibs on the shop's name, and I get to name the house, that means

Tommy will want to name our boat.' Her brow crinkled as her chip flopped. 'Will we still get a boat, do you think?'

'Hell yeah. And I trust the name of it with Tommy. In fact, if memory serves me correctly, he kind of already named the vessel.'

'Ooh, yes. When we were on Lexi's boat.'

'Hmm, you do know ours won't be as posh as that one, unless you want a smaller house.'

Harriet playfully placed a greasy finger on her temple and twisted her lips to one side. 'Hmm, house or boat. Let me see.'

'We could ditch the house idea and live on a boat.'

Her shoulders relaxed along with her smile. 'Ooh, wouldn't that be something. Sailing around the world. Stopping off in every port.'

'Something to add to our to-do list. Honeymoon, perhaps.'

Harriet flicked a chip his way as she laughed. 'Jude Jackson. You really do have it all planned out, don't you?'

'The only thing I don't have planned is how to eat this lump of fish without any cutlery.' He gazed around the floor by her crossed legs. 'Didn't you bring any?'

'You use your fingers.' She demonstrated by shoving a piece of battered cod into her mouth and licking her lips.

'Is this custom here?'

'Yep. When you don't have a knife and fork.' She laughed, making him laugh.

'Okay, well, know this, I've made another decision. This here is what we'll serve on our wedding day. How do you like that?'

'Lovely.' She beamed a smile through her food. 'My family will love you forever. Now, what's my surprise?'

'I'm putting your name on the deeds to this place. Now, we'll own it together. Officially.'

'Really?'

'Yeah. What do you think?'

'I think I love you.'

'That's good enough.'

Harriet's happy face told him everything he needed to know.

God, I love my life. And my future wife.

28

Harriet

Harriet couldn't tell if time was passing her by quickly or slowly, all she knew was her heart was skipping beats whilst she stood at the entrance to the brand-new hotel that belonged to the Renshaw family.

'Looks nice,' said Jude, giving her an encouraging smile.

'I've only ever known this place as two hotels. It got divided before my time. It used to be called the Inn on the Left. It was the one that did the best business. The other one was always a bit run down. It was called the Inn on the Right.'

Jude laughed out loud, and Harriet nudged his elbow. 'Well, come on. Seriously? That's what they named their hotels?'

Harriet hushed him, worried someone might overhear. 'Mum said there was a lot of anger over here. It's in the past now. The current Renshaws and Trents got married this year. Two brothers married two sisters, then they joined the hotel again.' She placed one hand on her chest and draped the other over Jude's arm. 'Isn't that a lovely story?'

'Got to love a happy ending.'

They shared a tender kiss in the doorway, then entered the foyer.

Jude gestured over to the open fireplace. 'If it were up to me, I would have stayed here. Looks cosy. Milly found Hotel Royale more to her taste. Not sure what Keaton would have picked. Knowing him, the pub.'

'I wonder how he's getting on. Have you had any more updates yet?'

Jude tapped his phone snuggled into the back pocket of his shorts. 'Yeah, same as before. He's improving every day, and Milly thinks Juliette is the main reason behind that. She says his whole face lights up every time Juliette walks in.' He kissed the top of Harriet's head and pulled her closer to his side. 'You did the right thing, Hal. You've changed his life.'

'I wouldn't go that far.' She approached the reception desk and asked the lady standing there for Elliot Renshaw. She turned back to Jude when the receptionist walked away. 'I think Keaton is changing his own life.'

'Give yourself some credit.'

She went to say something else, but Elliot appeared.

'Hi, Harriet. I heard you bought The Old Boat Clubhouse. My grandfather used to be part of the swimming club there when he was a young man. I figured you'd be round soon. You want to add your leaflet to our rack?' He pointed to some stacked flyers at the end of the counter, where the Donkey Sanctuary was poking out on the top tier.

'Well, yes and no.' She handed some leaflets to the receptionist, then turned back to Elliot. 'Erm, may we have a private word with you, please?'

His bright aquamarine eyes beamed straight at her, then over at Jude.

'Oh, this is my partner, Jude Jackson. I don't think you've met.' She gestured towards him, and the two men shook hands.

'I've heard about you, Jude. Not much stays secret around these parts. You were working for Keaton Byrd, right?'

Jude nodded and smiled as he gestured towards Harriet. 'Yeah, until I met this one. Now my whole life has changed.'

Elliot grinned widely. 'Yep, they get you like that, don't they?' He waved them to a back room. 'Come into my office.'

Swallowing hard and gripping Jude's hand a little too tightly, she followed the two men inside.

'So,' said Elliot, offering Harriet his comfy office chair, which she declined. 'What do you want to see me about? Oh, this isn't about Nora trying to arrange a fortieth birthday party for me, is it? I keep telling her I'm going to be thirty-eight. I don't know why she doesn't believe me.'

Harriet shook her head, then glanced at Jude to see if he'd fill in the blanks, but he didn't, so she caved and started talking. 'When we were fixing up the shop, we found some old letters beneath the floorboards. We weren't sure what to do with them because, well, you see, they're love letters written by your grandfather to Conway Trent.'

And breathe. Goodness, I hope I haven't destroyed Elliot's happy family memories. His face isn't giving much away. Oh, I want to run away. I feel really bad now.

'Can I see them?' asked Elliot, holding out a hand.

'Sure.' Harriet rummaged through her large shoulder bag. 'I'm sorry we read them, Elliot. We know they're private, but we didn't know at first, and we wanted to return them to a family member. My grandad told me Dusty was your grandfather.' She handed them over, trying hard to keep her hand steady. 'I hope I haven't made waves for your family with this info.'

Elliot perused the first letter whilst shaking his head slightly. 'No, don't be daft. It was what it was, at the end of the day. This isn't your fault. Besides, we'd heard the rumour our grandad had an affair with his best friend, but there were so many other rumours as to why their hotel got split in half, we didn't know what to believe.' He nodded at the letter he was browsing. 'I guess this clears things up.'

'I'm still sorry, Elliot,' said Harriet quietly.

'It's okay, Harriet. You haven't ruined any happy memories. I never had any. My family was a mess. Anyway, no one who this would affect is alive today, and Ned and I made peace with the two remaining Trents. Married them, in fact. So, all's good here.'

Harriet took a much-needed breath and was pleased Jude hadn't let go of her hand. 'I think it's lovely what you've done with the place, Elliot. Everyone is glad Pepper River Inn is back on the map.'

He smiled and placed the letters on his desk. 'Thanks. We're pleased too.'

'Okay, well, I'm glad that's sorted. I've been quite worried, but we'll let you get on. We have lots more leaflets to hand out. Hope to see you joining in some water sports activities soon.'

Elliot laughed, then leaned down to kiss her cheek before showing them out. 'I'll see what I can fit in. And thanks for the letters.'

'Good to meet you,' said Jude, shaking Elliot's hand once more.

Elliot pointed over to the entrance to the dining room. 'Come by one evening for dinner. It's on me.'

'Oh, you don't have to do that.' Harriet was already hungry just looking through the doorway. She'd eaten there before, but not often. The food was always nice, so she was happy to return.

Elliot followed them outside to the beautiful gardens recently created. 'Oh, please. It's the least I can do. You've solved a family mystery. Plus, you're probably stressed out building a new business. You could do with a night out. You stop by whenever you want, okay?'

Harriet gave him a quick hug. 'Thanks, Elliot. And good to see you. It's been a while.'

'Take care now,' he replied, waving them off.

Jude swung her arm up in the air. 'Well, that went better than you expected.'

'I do tend to overthink.'

He gasped dramatically and mocked shock horror. 'You, overthink? No way!'

She laughed and put her arm around his waist. 'Do you know what, Jude. I haven't actually felt too stressed out about building our business. Have you?'

'A little. I'm more settled now I have my visa and we have insurance. I'm more excited than anything.'

'Yes, that's how I feel. Sometimes, it feels a bit strange though. As if I'm in a dream or something. I can't believe how happy I am.'

Jude stopped them walking and stepped in front of her, holding her face. 'I'm going to make you even happier right now.'

She leaned forward for a kiss, but he pulled back.

'No, that's not what I meant, Hal. I have some good news.'

Lowering his hands and clasping them tightly to her chest, she urged him to spit it out.

Jude breathed out a laugh and kissed her knuckles. 'We got the land.'

It took a moment for the penny to drop. She gasped quietly, her lungs tightening from pure excitement. 'Really, Jude?'

'Yeah, baby. Coral Cottage is about to be born.'

Harriet leaped into his arms, forcing him to catch her and hold her up. Jude spun them around whilst she squealed into his neck. She gasped again and straightened. 'Oh, I've remembered something. I forgot to give Elliot the golden key. I left it in the tin back at the shop.'

'Never mind that. We can sort it another day. Right now, I'm thinking celebratory kiss, then back to our day job, then lunch by the harbour.'

'Another wonderful plan, Mr Jackson.'

29

Jude

The late-August sun was hot and the air humid for the annual RNLI Lifeboat Day. An excited Jude had dragged along a reluctant Harriet. There were way more people there than he had expected, not that it bothered him. The buzz was electric and seeing the lifeboats up close and personal was thrilling. Jude felt like a kid in a toy shop, and he wasn't about to hide that fact.

Harriet was mooching in the gift shop, so he took the opportunity to go and introduce himself to Finn Silver. He knew the man who he was searching for was thirty-five, medium built, with dark hair and dark eyes. He was also told Finn was a smaller-built version of Heath, and as Jude had already met the big brother, he had a good idea who he was looking for.

A man matching the description was standing over by a small gathering of people, having his picture taken. His bright yellow uniform and big smile stood out amongst the group. Jude waited for the family to finish taking photographs before heading over to say hello.

'Hey, Finn Silver? We spoke on the phone. I'm Jude Jackson.'

'Jude, hello, welcome.' Finn reached out to shake hands, then guided him over to a quiet corner of the station. 'You had a look around?'

'I can't stop looking around. I feel I belong here.'

Finn had a deep laugh that matched the gravel in his tone and crinkled the corners of his eyes. 'Doesn't look as though I need to pitch to you.'

'No, man. I'm already in. Just tell me where to sign.'

Finn waved over an older man. 'You can see Bert about that. But, just so you know, you will have to go through training first. It doesn't matter how much experience you already have with the water. If you want to be boat crew, you have got to train.'

'That's fine by me. And you're a firefighter as well?'

'Yeah, I work four day shifts. I also help on my dad's farm, where I live. And when I have time, I volunteer over here. You can let us know what days and hours you have free. We don't expect you to give up your day job. This is about us all fitting in where we can. You'll be on call at the times you're available. There are quite a lot of us. It's needed.'

Jude watched the grey-haired man approaching them from the other side of the station. He was stopping off along the way to meet and greet visitors and friends. 'And you rely heavily on donations?'

'Yep.'

'But your country is an island.'

'Yep.'

'Seems odd.'

Finn laughed. 'Yep.'

'Well, I can't wait to join. My partner's not so keen. She wants me to work in your gift store.'

'You can, if you want. We have all sorts of roles here. It's not just boat crew that makes the RNLI.'

Jude pointed over to the sea. 'I want to be out there, Finn. Sometimes I feel as if the water is part of me.'

'Oh, you're one of those.'

Jude laughed as he turned back to him. 'What does that mean?'

'Water baby.'

'Sums me up. I learned a lot about safety in the water when I was a kid. I don't just want to have a water sports business, I want to teach people about rips and how to float. How to swim, even.'

'Everyone should know how to swim. It's important.'

Jude nodded. 'I have classes booked in over at the swimming pool at the leisure centre. I've got a school bringing pupils over during October, now I've proven I don't have a criminal record and I'm a decent citizen. My mother had to send documents over from America. I feel as though I have documents coming out of my ears at the moment. I'm hoping, by putting down roots here, I'll be allowed to sign up with you guys. I want to help save lives. Anyone can get into trouble. Even me. The ocean is a whole other world, and if I can help educate people on how to stay as safe as possible when in the water, that's what I want to do. Someone taught me. Now it's my turn to pass on the knowledge and skills I have.'

Finn patted him on the back. 'You have a good attitude. You ever think about joining the fire brigade?'

Jude breathed out a laugh. 'Nope. No fire, thank you very much. Just water for me.'

'Hey, sometimes we rescue cats from trees. There's lots of variety.'

Bert finally managed to reach them, and Finn introduced Jude as their newest recruit, which made Bert chuckle with delight.

'Step this way, Jude. Let's talk shop,' said Bert, opening a door.

Jude happily handed over his CV. 'I brought this, just in case.'

'Brilliant,' said Bert. 'Come on, close the door behind you. This is just an informal chat, so don't look so nervous.'

Jude laughed. 'These are excited nerves.'

I have to act cool. This guy is gonna think I'm nuts if I start fanboying him, and I am totally fanboying that uniform. I wonder how long I have to train for? I hope it's not too long. I want to get started straight away. Okay, Jude, get a grip. Listen to what the man's saying.

Harriet rolled her eyes dramatically as Jude left Bert's office and sprinted towards her to blurt out in record speed everything she needed and didn't need to know about him signing up.

'Okay, Jude. You need to lay off the sugar. Did you eat a whole bag of candyfloss?'

'What? No. I haven't eaten anything. I've been too pumped to eat. Although, I reckon I could go for a burger now. Can you smell that? Mmm, it's wafting over here from somewhere around here.'

Harriet pointed behind her. 'Burger van up the road. Come on, let's go eat, then you can tell me more about how you'll be training to risk your own life.'

Jude's shoulders slumped along with his smile. 'Ah, come on, Hal. Don't rain on my parade. You know how much I want this.'

Harriet pursed her lips, then smiled softly, drawing him in for a hug. 'Sorry. I'm just worried. I don't want to lose you. I've only just found you.'

'Hey, I'm not going anywhere. Please, try to think more positively.'

'It's hard, Jude. I'm not used to this much joy. I keep thinking it's going to vanish.'

He kissed her cheek, trying hard to reassure her insecurities. It was a challenge he was coming to understand, but she couldn't help the way she felt, so all he could do was tell her over and over how everything was going to be okay. Not that he had a crystal ball or anything, but he had great faith. He wished it would rub off onto her.

'I love you, Harriet. You've got to have some trust in our future, okay?'

A quiet huff came from her direction as she moved to his side so they could walk over to the food vans parked up by the main road. 'Okay, but I'm probably going to have a lot of questions about the RNLI.'

'That's cool. I have a question for you.'

'What's that?'

'What the hell is candyfloss?'

She pointed over to a lady spinning some onto a stick.

'Cotton candy. That's what you guys call it over here? I didn't know that.'

Harriet eyed up the pink sugary fluff. 'I've always fancied having a go. Seems simple enough, doesn't it? Swirl the stick around the machine. Job done.' She giggled into his arm. 'I bet I'd get into a right old pickle. I can see myself in A&E covered in candyfloss, having nurses save me by licking my arm.'

'Hey, no one's licking your arm but me.'

'We'll get some after lunch.'

'Is that your way of saying you want me to lick your arm?'

Harriet leaned into his side, causing him to stumble and then rebalance. She flinched as he attempted to lick her bare shoulder, catching his nose in the strap of her pink sundress.

They messed about, tickling each other and laughing all the way to the burger van, where they only stopped to order some food. A bench became available, so they quickly plopped themselves down to eat before someone else came along and sat there.

Jude rested his back on the wooden slats, eating his lunch whilst enjoying the sun on his face. He pulled his sunglasses from his head and watched Harriet do the same. All in all, it had been a great day, and it wasn't over yet. Sitting quietly in the sun, with the woman he loved, watching the calm waves rolling to shore in the near distance soothed every part of him. His adrenaline rush from being up close and personal to a lifeboat had settled, and now he was simply content to sit in companionable silence with Harriet, watching the world pass them by.

A paper napkin was passed his way as Harriet removed the scrunched wrapper the burger came in. She tossed the rubbish into the bin next to the bench, then handed him a bottle of cola. Something about her simple act made him feel as though they had been with each other way longer than one summer. He had a moment where he laughed to himself at his life.

I'm in England. What the hell! In May, I was scooping Keaton off the floor at the Platinum Stars Ball. Three months later, and I'm sitting on a bench, eating lunch after finding out how to join a rescue team. In another country. I've bought a business, a piece of land, I'm about to buy a boat, and I've fallen in love.

He knew life could be mind-blowing at times. He was definitely blown away.

I can't believe how happy I am. Was I really that unhappy before? How crazy.

'Shall we head back now, Jude? I promised Tommy a swim later on.'

'Sure. Can I give him his new surfboard yet? It's killing me it's sitting in the storage hut, waiting to be used. I can't wait to see his face.'

'You're not to spoil him.'

He offered out his hand as he stood, the flow of happiness filling him once more as her small hand slid perfectly into his. 'Come on, Hal. It's a surfboard. He has to have one. I bought it for him. I can't hold out much longer.'

'I think you're more excited than he'll be when he finds out.'

'So, that's a yes then?'

She groaned, faking annoyance, then smiled as they headed back to their car. 'Yes. You can bring it to the beach later on with us.'

'Ooh, do you think we should buy one of those cute beach huts? They really are something, aren't they?'

Harriet breathed out a laugh through her nose. 'No. We're not buying anything else. I'm starting to worry about you and money.'

'Blame Keaton. He spoiled me way more than my parents. I guess I kind of got used to living the high life. Whenever he wanted anything, he got it.'

'Well, you're not Keaton Byrd, so reel it in, mister. We've got a home to build.'

'Let's go stand on our land.'

'And do what?'

'Nothing. We'll just stand there.'

Harriet chuckled, making him join in. 'Okay, hubby-to-be, let's go stand on our land and admire all the dirt we own.'

Jude lifted his free hand, circling it above his head, almost slapping a passer-by in the face. 'Hey, born in manure, come up smelling like roses.'

Harriet crinkled her nose. 'I hope our house doesn't smell like manure.'

They both laughed at the thought, then shared a kiss, smiling onto each other's lips at their joy.

Finally, life with Keaton was a distant memory.

30

Harriet

The beach was packed, thanks to the glorious sunshine and the summer school holiday. Tommy was happily showing off his new surfboard to one of his friends, Kasey, by the shoreline as Harriet shared some pleasantries with the child's stepmum, Belle, Ned Renshaw's wife, and previous Trent family member. She made sure she avoided talk of the love letters she had handed over to Elliot. Instead, she spoke about more present matters, shamelessly promoting her business.

I should be chatting normally. I wonder what she thinks. Jude calls this networking. I call it getting on people's nerves.

Belle listened politely, but Harriet quickly changed the subject, believing she couldn't talk shop every time she bumped into someone. It seemed rude, in her opinion, but she did need to drum up some business. The Old Boat Clubhouse had an opening day coming up.

Harriet glanced at Tommy, who seemed to be doing a better job at advertising than her, as Kasey quickly demonstrated by running up to Belle to ask for a surfboard and lessons.

Belle went to reply but stopped, frowned, and squinted out to sea. 'Is that someone in trouble?'

Harriet quickly scanned the waves at the same time Jude stood from faffing about with his own surfboard.

Out in the distance, a boy was bobbing up and down with one arm frantically waving in the air each time he came back to the surface.

Before Harriet had a chance to respond, a scream ripped through the air, coming from the drowning lad's mother.

Jude ran into the water, diving over waves, going straight into the butterfly stroke. Harriet watched him change to the front crawl, powering through the water as though he were auditioning for *Baywatch*.

A man close by was on the phone to the coastguard, and Harriet prayed they would hurry, because she could see the rip the boy was trapped in, and her heart was in her throat as Jude swam directly into the area.

Oh God, this is it. Jude's going to die. I knew this was all too good to be true. No one's allowed this much happiness, surely. He's going to be taken from me. This is the moment it all comes crashing down.

Harriet had tried so hard to be happy, but something kept niggling at her. Making her wary. Thinking it all a dream. The kind that didn't happen to her. She wasn't used to things working out for her.

Oh, please don't let him die. Please don't take Jude away from me. I can't bear it. I can't watch.

She took a step closer to the water.

I need to get out there. No, it's not safe. Tommy needs me. Oh, bloody hell.

'Look, Mum. Jude's moving to the side. He knows what to do.' Tommy was pressing up onto his toes, trying for a better view.

The child's mother was screaming out pointless instructions, which only irritated Harriet. They locked eyes for a split second, and Harriet made sure her face revealed every ounce of anger she was feeling.

'It's that Digby kid,' said Belle, shading her eyes with one hand. 'He's in the year above my Kasey. It would help your fella if the kid stopped whacking him in the face.'

Flipping Digby! That kid will be the death of me. I swear to God, if his mum doesn't stop shouting at Jude, I'm going to whack her.

Belle leaned closer to Harriet. 'I know she's worried, but he's saving her kid. Look, he's doing a great job. There's no need for all that swearing. What's your partner's name?'

'Jude.'

Belle yelled out to sea, gaining some attention. 'Go on, Jude. You've got this.' She flicked back her long blonde hair and grinned widely at Harriet.

Suddenly, the RNLI came into view, and it wasn't long before Jude and Digby were pulled into the boat.

'About time,' shouted Digby's mum, who then quickly approached Harriet with a face full of thunder. 'Your stupid boyfriend could have killed my son. Don't think anyone will be signing up to your water sports courses. I'll make sure of that.'

What? Is she nuts?

Without even realising what she was doing, Harriet swung her arm to punch the woman straight in the face, but Belle caught her movement mid-swing, taking charge of the moment.

'Look, lady, Jude saved your boy.' Belle held her arms out to all the witnesses up on their feet, watching the scene. 'He's a hero. You, however, might want to think about how on earth your son ended up that far out to sea in the first place. He's seven. You should have eyes on him at all times. And teach him what the flags on the beach mean.'

'Don't you blame me,' snapped Digby's mum, squaring up to Belle. 'You can't watch kids twenty-four seven. That man should never have gone in. Digby would have been fine waiting for the RNLI to show up.'

Harriet scoffed, almost choking on her own saliva. 'Oh, yeah, he was doing so well. Poor little sod, and that's coming from me, who doesn't even like him.'

'What's wrong with my kid?'

'He's a flipping headache, that's what.'

'Oh, yeah, you should look at your own son.'

Harriet glanced at Tommy, who simply glanced back. Rage and hellfire consumed her, and it took every ounce of willpower she had not to reach out and throttle the scowling woman flapping her arms in front of her. 'There's nothing wrong with my kid, thank you very much. Yours, however, is a bullying little—'

'Okay, ladies,' interrupted Belle, standing closer between them. 'Let's tone it down. The beach is full of children.' She nodded towards where the lifeboat was coming in. 'Why don't you go see your son.'

'Yeah, and don't come back,' mumbled Harriet.

'How about you all mind your own business,' said Digby's mum, turning in the golden sand, crushing someone's sandcastle. She glared once more at Harriet. 'I feel sorry for your kid, what with all the men coming and going in his life. Yeah, I've seen you in the papers. Can't decide who you want to sleep with, eh?'

Harriet practically jumped on her but was held off by a rather strong Belle. 'You what?' she screamed, flapping her arms over Belle's, desperately wanting to get at Digby's smirking mother.

The woman wobbled her way across the sand whilst Belle let go of Harriet.

Tommy reached up for his mum's hand. 'Mum, it's all right. She's gone now.'

222

'Did Digby drown?' asked Kasey, tugging at Belle's shorts.

'No. He's fine. Thanks to Jude.' Belle nodded over to the small crowd by the lifeboat in the near distance.

'He should have floated on his back,' said Tommy to Kasey. 'That's what you do when you're caught in a rip.'

Belle nudged Harriet's elbow, bringing her out of her death glare with the back of Digby's mum's head. 'I'm so glad Jude will be teaching water safety lessons at the swimming pool next month. What a relief it will be for a lot of parents. It's one thing for us to teach them, but you know what kids are like. They tend to listen more to teachers than us. Plus, I heard he's going to hand out certificates and badges. The kids will love that.'

Yeah, she's right. I'm not focusing on stupid Digby and his ignorant mother any longer. I need to see Jude. I can't believe he saved someone's life. Oh, goodness, then he got saved by the RNLI.

She laughed on the inside.

That will go down well with the station. Let's get over there.

She said goodbye to Belle and Kasey and picked up Jude's surfboard whilst Tommy carried his own.

Jude was laughing about something with Finn, and Digby had already been given the all-clear and had bounced back quite nicely. His mother was yelling at him to come over to her, but he was busy telling a group of boys about his epic swimming abilities and how he had to save a man's life.

Harriet was glad the infuriating woman had buggered off. She made a mental note to let one of the local reporters know what really happened so they could write the story in the paper, letting everyone know Jude was a hero.

I can't have anyone trying to destroy what we're building. That nasty woman could spit her venom anywhere and everywhere.

She quickly sent a text to a number a reporter had given her back when she was seen hanging out with Keaton. She was so over fake news. Jude's smiling eyes met hers as she raised them from her phone.

So, he thinks he can give me his doe-eyed look, and I'll fall into his arms after he gave me a flipping heart attack.

Harriet's shaking finger pointed over at Digby. 'Well, he seems fine,' she snapped, dropping the surfboard to the sand, which caused Jude to frown before widening his eyes her way.

'Yes, I'm okay too, thanks for asking.'

'Fine too! Fine too! I'll give you fine too. You scared the living daylights out of me, Jude Jackson. I thought… I thought…' Harriet gulped in warm salty air, clutching her throat as her chest tightened. 'I… I…'

Jude wrapped his arms around her, pulling her close to his damp wetsuit. A gentle kiss was placed on her temple followed by another to her cheek. 'I'm okay, Hal. I knew what I was doing. I'm a trained lifeguard.'

She pulled back, knowing full well everyone who was looking could see her watery eyes. 'I just wasn't prepared for that.'

He breathed out a small laugh and lowered his forehead to rest upon hers. 'Nobody is.'

'Oh, Jude, I thought you were going to drown. I thought all our plans were over before they'd even started. I thought—'

'You think too much.' He pulled her back for another hug. 'I think we need to get in the water and start surfing.'

She jolted away. 'What, after that?'

224

'Yep. There's no reason not to carry on with our day, Harriet. The kid's fine, our boy is looking forward to trying out his new board, and we're not afraid of the sea. Plus, the waves are small. Perfect for Tommy.'

'Yes!' cheered Tommy, standing on his board whilst pointing out to the water.

Well, I guess this is my life. Two adrenaline junkies, water sports galore, and a partner who goes around saving lives.

Gulping down another whoosh of warm air, Harriet smiled weakly at her boy. 'Go on then.'

She watched Jude say his goodbyes to the lifeboat crew, knowing full well he would have preferred to head off with them to find some other poor soul lost in the waves or stranded on some rocks.

Jude took his board under his arm, gestured towards the shore, and slipped his free hand into Harriet's, acting as though it was just another day where no drama took place.

'Hey, Hal,' he said quietly, guiding her through the sunbathers. 'I love you.'

She warmed immediately but tried not to show her face, as she was sure it held a tint of blush. 'My heart's still racing, you know.'

'Yeah, I'll make it race even more tonight.' He smiled out to sea, but she saw his cheeky wink.

'Jude, how can you be so calm after what happened?'

He tilted his board, holding one end on the sand, and turned her way. 'Because, my beautiful lady, everything is okay. You need to breathe, relax, and not dwell.'

Harriet relaxed her shoulders as best she could whilst still feeling tense and in need of a holiday. 'How do you make life look so easy?'

He shrugged, looking as though he was actually mulling over an answer. 'I'm happy. And if there's nothing going on to make me feel the opposite, then, I guess, I'm gonna stay in my zone.'

'You have a zone?'

He nodded to the small rolling waves washing up to their feet. 'I did stress for years, Hal. Since being here with you, I'm back. The water, you and Tommy, this life we've started, that's my zone, and there's nothing in this world that's gonna pull me out.'

Finally, an easy breath left Harriet's lungs, and she snuggled into his side. 'Aww, Jude, you say the loveliest things.'

He met her gaze and smiled warmly. 'My life has changed, Harriet, and so has yours. Let's enjoy what we have. No worries. No regrets. And lots of memories to make. One day, we'll be like your grandfather, and when that time comes, I want to look back and be able to say I enjoyed my life, and I got to know what love truly feels like.'

'I love you, Jude.'

'This is just the beginning, Hal. We're gonna have a blast.'

She smiled as he dropped his board and carried her into the sea, planting kisses on her cheek along the way.

31

Jude

The small changing room Jude had built in The Old Boat Clubhouse was getting full use once the swimming club turned up for their first group swim, thanks to Tessie spreading the word.

There was only a small gathering, but Jude was still pleased with the turnout. There was Tessie and her friend from the book shop, Anna, and Belle brought her husband, Ned, who was a keen swimmer. Jude, Harriet, and Finn made up the rest of the club.

Nowhere in the world did Jude feel calm and exhilarated at the same time as he did when swimming in the sea. The cold water waking every fibre of his being, and the space around and beneath him keeping his soul soothed to the point of everlasting peace.

He ploughed through the dark waves, flipping over into the backstroke, then back to front crawl, glancing over at the shallow shoreline every so often to keep an eye on the least experienced swimmers in the group, Anna and Belle.

Tessie was swimming further out than him, alongside Finn, and it didn't take long for Jude to notice that Ned had Olympic-swimmer skills, even if he was staying close to the shallow end, which Jude knew was because of Belle.

The thought of charging his new club money for a hot drink at The Old Boat Clubhouse afterwards was the only thing niggling at him in the water. He floated on his back for a while, taking in the early morning sky.

Not sure this is a money-maker. They're my friends, and it's only a tea or coffee. I can't take their cash. Oh well, never mind. It's a small thing, and my new customers will make use of the coffee machine, which reminds me. I have to fix that drain behind the hut, or whatever that gungy thing is. Oh, and I need to ask Dolly from the gift shop if she has any ribbon to wrap over the door for opening day tomorrow.

He rolled over and started a slow breaststroke, smiling because his business was set to go.

Shame we missed spring and summer this year, but we've got plenty to be getting on with, and come next year, we'll be knee-deep in customers and students. I can't believe I actually have my own wetsuit brand. Boat Clubhouse could become a household name, one day.

He changed direction, heading towards the shore, where Harriet was swimming close to Ned. He wanted to swim by her side for a bit, but knew she didn't favour going out as far as he was, no matter how confident she was.

'Hey,' she said, spitting seawater from her lips. 'I was thinking we should get flags for this end of the beach. They don't have any in the bay.'

'Great idea. It's only a small beach, but worth putting up flags if we spot any danger.'

Harriet flopped her arms on his shoulders and pushed her body into his. 'I wish we were on our own, because I really want you, right here, in the water.'

He laughed onto her lips as they pressed onto his. 'I'm sure we can arrange that for another time. Swimming club is only one morning a week. We have the rest to ourselves.'

Harriet wrapped her legs around him, pulling them lower to the tips of the gentle waves.

'Behave yourself, Hal. We've got company.' He kissed her hard before pulling back, gesturing for her to swim with him. They both went into a power-swim, leaving all stress and to-do lists behind for a few more minutes, then headed back to the hut to warm up.

Harriet handed him a towel and started making hot drinks for everyone. 'I'm going into work in a bit. What you got planned this morning, Jude?'

'I want to finish clearing out back, then get ready for the opening tomorrow. Should be a big turnout. I hope.' He glanced at Tessie, who was about to enter the changing room. 'Tess has pretty much told everyone on the island. I'm not sure we'll all fit out front.' He laughed quietly along with Harriet, then whispered his decision not to charge the swimming club any money for drinks.

She agreed and handed him a coffee. 'I'll pop back after my shift at the hotel. I'll bring lunch, okay?'

'Sounds good.'

* * *

There was some sort of gunky black hole around the back of the hut, and Jude presumed it was once a working drain of some sort.

Armed with a bucket and a whole heap of nice-smelling chemicals, Jude bent to a folded towel in front of the cesspit. He put on some blue rubber gloves, wrinkled his nose at the smell coming from the ground, and reluctantly placed one hand into the abyss.

'Oh good Lord, save me now.'

It was a lot deeper than he thought, and something felt slimy even with gloves on. His fingertips met with something hard, so he shuffled his hand around to see where the walls of the pit were. A square-shaped hole was what he was making out by touch alone, as he couldn't see anything beneath the sludgy gloom.

'What is that?' he mumbled, leaning closer.

He gripped something and, against his better judgement, twisted and turned the item, trying hard to lift it out.

Suddenly, it became unstuck, causing Jude to jolt back as his hand came flying out of the hole. A blob of gloop hit him straight in the face, bringing with it a pungent smell of death and an instant churn of Jude's guts.

'Oh, fail my life. I think I've caught the plague. And what is this?' He placed the box on the ground and proceeded to clean off the gunk as best he could, as it seemed to be part of the metal exterior.

A keyhole came into view, and something immediately told Jude to fetch the golden key that still hadn't been handed over to the Renshaws. Only because they had forgotten about it altogether, what with everything going on.

He quickly went inside and plonked the box into the sink, then removed one glove to hunt down the key.

'Where did Harriet put it? I'm sure it was under the sink.' He rummaged around, then found it stashed away behind a packet of bourbon biscuits in the top cupboard above a stack of bodyboards.

Aha!

He daren't run the tap water over the box in case it seeped inside and ruined anything that might have survived its last ordeal, so he used some kitchen paper to wipe over the side where the keyhole was.

A small amount of adrenaline flipped his heart when the key appeared to fit the lock. 'Ooh, please be hidden treasure. This is England. There has to be medieval coins or a queen's crown. Hello, mystery box. What do you hold inside?' He let out a quiet *Mwah ha-ha* sound, entertaining himself, then turned the key.

'Ooh, it worked. Okay, let's see what we have here. It better not be a dead rat. God, I hate rats.' He shivered, then opened the lid.

Inside was a smaller box, and Jude wondered if it was going to be some sort of Russian doll game. He lifted out the smaller box and removed the lid to find two letters wrapped in some sort of plastic sandwich bag.

He released them of their stale, smelly prison and the stupid part of him took a sniff.

'Whoa! That is not good.'

He homed in on the blurry writing on the top letter, then looked on the front of the other one.

'Dusty and Conway, we meet again.' He chewed the side of his gum for a second, pondering over reading his find.

Oh, come on, Jude. You so know you're reading them.

'Sorry, guys, but I need to know if you have an ending to your story.' He placed one finger to his lips, doing a shushing action until he realised it smelled like the old letters, so dropped his hand from his face.

He sat in the chair behind the counter and opened the one addressed to Conway.

My dearest Conway.

I don't know if you will ever receive this letter, as I know you are dying. I can't see you, but oh, how I wish I could. All these years, all this time, you have lived within my heart. It's breaking me you are right next door and I cannot sit at your bedside to comfort you when you most need me.

I love you. You are my Con, and forever will be. I brought this here because this is our place. When we were out there swimming together, we were truly free of the lives we were living. I know we've been unfair to our wives all these years, but I've never been strong enough to let you go.

When you're gone, I'm going to come with you. I'll meet your soul in the sea, where we belonged. I pray you get a day when you can come to the clubhouse one last time. I'll leave this here, just in case.

I don't want to live in a world where you no longer exist. We should have sailed away when we were young. What fools we have been.

I'll be seeing you, Con.

Lost in you always. D

Jude inhaled a shaky breath and rolled back the tear that had found its way into his eye. He swallowed the hard lump in his throat and carefully placed the letter upon the counter so he could read the other one.

Dusty, I'm here.

I asked to be taken here one last time. They don't know why. Only we know why. This will probably be the last time I leave my bed. I wish you were lying beside me every night. Those precious moments I shared with you throughout our lives made everything bearable. I know we're selfish, but you are my drug, my air, my world. I can't bring myself to let Etti down. She's been a good wife to me all these years.

I have my sons. You have yours. I'm sure we'll be punished somehow for our love. Although, I feel living a lie has been my daily punishment. I'm dying, my love. This is my time for regrets. I regret not telling my wife I loved you more. I regret not sailing away with you all those years ago, and I regret not holding you each and every day.

Do not join me before your time, Dusty. I want you to live the rest of your life remembering us, so I can live on in you for a while longer.

I hope you come back here and read this. The Old Boat Clubhouse is my favourite place in the whole world. If you can find a way to sprinkle my ashes in the sea right here, I'll smile from my place of peace. I'm not opposed to you sneaking in my hotel and snatching them, if needs must. This is where I want to be. Try. Just try, for me.

Lost in you always. Con.

A tear fell down Jude's cheek. He wiped it away, sniffed, and stared over at the door, knowing where Dusty and Conway felt their freedom and love was right outside.

Jeez, I need to call Harriet. I want to hold her. Tell her how much I love her.

He took a breath and picked up his phone. There was someone else he needed to speak to first. 'Hello, Ned. I found some more letters.'

32

Harriet

The opening day for The Old Boat Clubhouse had finally arrived, and Harriet was way more excited than she thought she would be. It wasn't just the day that felt surreal. Her whole life had changed so drastically in one summer, and she couldn't be happier, even more so because her son was full of joy.

Tommy stood at the front of the gathering as Harriet held up a red strip of ribbon for Jude to cut. As soon as it spilt into two, one piece floating over Harriet's head, Tommy ran towards the new water sports shop, sprinting inside to grab his bodyboard.

Lots of hugs and kisses were handed out, along with fizzy wine, orange juice, and seafood. The sun was shining, the seagulls were singing their song, and the whole of Pepper Bay and most of Sandly had turned up for the big event.

Harriet managed to pull Jude to one side, tugging him into the back part of the farm shop. She gave him a quick peck on the lips and smiled. 'Oh, I can't believe any of this, Jude. What a surprise this summer has been. I'm so glad you came to the Isle of Wight on your silly mission to clean up Keaton. Well, it worked. Not the way you planned, but he's in rehab, and you're here, with me. I did not see that one coming.'

Jude breathed out a laugh. 'Neither did I.'

'Look. I received a message this morning from Keaton. I wanted to show you after we opened.' Harriet whipped out her phone from the back pocket of her denim shorts and snuggled closer under Jude's arm so they could read it together.

Hey. What can I say to you that would be enough? You really did change my life. I still can't believe I'm back home. Home, of all places, and I have you to thank for that. Making me contact Juliette, pushing me forward, sending me to rehab. I don't have any more to add.

I want you to know I'm doing okay. Juliette has been great. She hasn't changed at all. She's still so beautiful inside and out, and I fall in love with her that little bit more each day.

I hope things are working out with surfer dude. I always knew he was destined for better things. God knows he paid his dues hanging out with me.

Hey, maybe I'll come visit one day. I'll bring Juliette to meet you both. Let her check out my ex-girlfriend, ha!

Seriously, you were an angel sent to me from I don't know who, but you and your little island saved me. I'll always be grateful. Reach out if you ever need my help with anything. I'll always have a soft spot for you and Jude.

Oh, and that extra nought at the end of the money I gave you wasn't done by accident. Enjoy your life, Harriet Hadley.

I'm gonna close now. You take care.

Harriet and Jude shared a smile.

'Hey, Hal. I asked Ned about his grandfather's ashes, and he said he believes they were placed with his grandmother, and Belle said she didn't know where her grandfather's ashes were.' He pulled her closer. 'When it's my time, we need to make sure everyone knows I want my ashes to go into the sea. Right here, Harriet. Our happy place.'

'Ooh, I like that idea. I'm going there too. I hope we'll always be together. I'm so glad we don't have a relationship we have to hide anymore. It's no way to live.'

They kissed until Tessie approached to pull them back to their guests.

Harriet beamed happily at the gathering and at her new life. It wasn't long ago Lexi had told her to take more risks.

How I ever said yes to Keaton Byrd, I'll never know, but I'm so glad I did. What a domino effect that action caused. I don't care if I never took risks before. I did this time. I got Jude. I knew men like him existed, and now I have my own.

She smiled, as Jude winked her way from the other side of the crowd. He wasn't shy about showing his love for her in front of everyone, and she liked that about him. There wasn't anything she didn't like about him. He brought air to her sails and gave her the stability she needed for Tommy.

The sea was calm and looked oh so refreshing. Harriet wanted to swim. Conway and Dusty materialised before her as she stood along the shoreline, staring out at the horizon. They were swimming, smiling, relaxing.

'Harriet, I want to show you something,' said Ned, approaching. He stood by her side and handed over a framed photograph. 'I thought you might like to see this. I just showed Jude. He wants to put it up behind the counter.'

She looked at the black-and-white picture of eight men, all somewhere between twenty and forty in age, she guessed. They were grouped together, wearing swim shorts and nothing else.

'It's the first swimming club from The Old Boat Clubhouse.' Ned pointed at a tall man at the back. His shoulders were broad, but his frame slim. 'That's my grandad.' Then, he moved his finger to a man in front of Dusty. 'That's Conway Trent.'

Harriet smiled warmly at the medium-built man, who had fair hair and cheeky glint in his eye. Her hand rested over her heart as thoughts of them standing where she stood washed over her. 'Oh, Ned. It's a sad story all round, isn't it?'

He gave a slight shrug and pursed his lips. 'Yeah, I guess it is.'

She followed his bright aquamarine eyes out to sea, then watched his chest rise and fall steadily. 'The sea holds many ghosts,' she whispered.

'That's what they say.'

Harriet tapped his arm. 'Do you want us to keep the picture here, Ned? It's up to you. I'm happy to. I think it's a nice touch. We'll have to have a photo done of our swimming group. I'll put that up as well. We'll have a wall especially for all the swimming clubs that come here.'

Ned turned her way and smiled. 'Yeah, sounds perfect.' He handed her the picture, then headed back to wrap his arm around his wife.

Harriet watched Jude walk towards her. She tilted the old photo his way. 'How about that, eh?'

'Oh, it's great, isn't it? We'll need one of our group as well.'

'That's what I said.' She leaned into him and sighed. 'The water is calling me, Jude. I'm happy everyone is here, celebrating with us, but I'll be glad when they're gone, and we can go for a swim.'

'Or when our boat arrives.'

Harriet laughed. 'Did you really buy a boat?'

'Of course. It was on the to-do list.'

She kissed his cheek and smiled. 'We're so lucky, aren't we?'

'Yep.'

'Of all the people I had to meet, I met another water baby.'

'Actually. You met a movie star first.'

Harriet breathed out a laugh as she stepped back to view him in full. 'Erm, actually, I think you'll find I met you first. In the lift, remember?'

He smiled, stepped forward, and placed his hands on her elbows. 'You smelled sweet, tropical. You made me think of the ocean.'

'I trod on your foot.'

'Yes, I remember that too.'

'That was our meet-cute.'

'Do they always feel awkward?'

Harriet giggled and glanced back up at the shop. 'You'd have to ask Lexi. She writes romance.'

'Well, whatever you want to call it, I'm glad it happened to us.' He kissed her lips and nuzzled his nose into her hair by her ear. 'Harriet Hadley, if only you knew how much your natural scent drives me wild.'

'I do now.' She pulled his face around so she could meet his lips again. 'I'm so happy, Jude,' she mumbled between kisses.

'Good.'

Her muffled laugh caused him to laugh back. 'I really want to see you wipe-out one day.'

Jude stepped back and playfully huffed. 'Oh, is that right?'

'I just know you fall off your surfboard. You probably do it on purpose so you can be back in the water.'

He laughed out loud, glancing at the gentle waves, and before Harriet could say another word, he removed the photograph from her, placed it on a nearby towel, leaped forward, threw her over his shoulder, and ran into the sea.

Harriet screamed with laughter as she came splashing into the cold water, with Jude falling to her side. They were soaked through and completely happy. She tossed some water his way, then sheltered her face with her arm as some came her way from him. He grabbed her again, dipping her low to the tips of an incoming wave. It rolled over her hair, removing any traces of the curled hairstyle she'd turned up with that morning.

Tommy was suddenly by their sides, splashing around whilst singing something about pirates.

Harriet and Jude sat in the sea by the shoreline and held on to each other tightly.

'If I were a pirate, you would be my treasure,' said Jude softly.

Harriet pulled back and took in his wet lashes and flushed cheeks. 'If you were a pirate, I would be your ship, sailing you only to this island.'

'That's fine by me. I don't want to be anywhere else.' Jude glanced over at the land. 'I didn't even know Pepper Bay existed.'

Harriet watched him laugh to himself. 'It's lovely here.'

There was nothing but pure warmth in Jude's face as he smiled her way. 'It sure is.'

She went to say something else, but all her sisters ran into the sea, splashing around her, pulling her to her feet, and making her laugh.

Jude picked her up, spinning her around, sheltering her from the flicks of water coming her way. He moved her along the shoreline, away from the chaos in the sea caused by the Hadleys.

Harriet felt her feet sink lower into the soft seabed beneath her drenched sandals. She smiled at the gentleness of the foam around their ankles as the cool liquid rolled to and from the shore.

'Hey, Harriet.' Jude cupped her face, bringing it up towards his own. 'Thank you.'

'What for?'

'Making me part of your life.'

Harriet breathed out a short laugh and placed her hands over his. 'This is so different to your last life.'

'Yeah, this one's way more exciting.'

'More than the razzle dazzle of film stars?'

Jude gave a half-shrug and brought his mouth close to hers. 'I've got a clubhouse full of stories, a whole heap of Hadleys, and I'm surrounded by the sea.'

'Well, that does sound exciting.'

'Sounds perfect, Harriet.' He kissed the tip of her nose and smiled. 'Every bit as perfect as you.'

Harriet gave him a quick peck on the lips, then tickled his ribs and brought him crashing down into the water. She rolled over him as he flipped on his back, laughing and grabbing at her waist. They tumbled around in the small waves lapping at the shore, then flopped to their backs and squinted up at the clear blue sky. Their hands linked on top of the shingles, crunching deeply into the coolness of the stones, then they turned to look at each other and smiled a smile filled with love, faith, and hope.

'Lost in you always, Jude Jackson,' she whispered.

He raised her hand and kissed her palm. 'Lost in you always, Harriet.'

* * *

If you enjoyed Harriet's story, come back and meet her sister Ashley.

Castle on the Mead

Harrison Connell leads a quiet life, but Ashley Hadley is determined to get him to come out of his shell. When she gets the chance to move into his castle, she sets about putting the old building back on the map. Harrison doesn't want his home to become a tourist attraction, but that's the least of his worries, as someone seems determined to destroy him, or maybe it's Ashley they want to hurt.

Ingram Content Group UK Ltd.
Milton Keynes UK
UKHW010643270723
425883UK00004B/282